# MAFIA'S FINAL PLAY

## MAFIA'S OBSESSION BOOK 3

### SUMMER COOPER

D1715990

**An Amazon Top 100**
A 5-book billionaire romance box set
Filthy Rich
Summer's other box sets include:
Too Much To Love
Down Right Dirty

**Mafia's Obsession**
A hot mafia romance series
Mafia's Dirty Secret
Mafia's Fake Bride
Mafia's Final Play

**Screaming Demons**
An MC romance series full of suspense
*Take Over*
Rough Start
Rough Ride
Rough Choice
*New Era*
Rough Patch
Rough Return
Rough Road
*New Territory*

Rough Trip
Rough Night
Rough Love

Check out Summer's entire collection at
**www.summercooper.com/books**

Happy reading,
Summer Cooper
xoxo

# ACKNOWLEDGMENTS

I'd like to give special thanks to

**Savvy**
who's helped me get the books out to the
world.

**Terri and Tasha**
for being the best and most supportive
editing team.

**Jenny**
for designing this book cover.

**My family**
for being supportive and believing in my
dreams.

Last but not least
My ARC Team
My Readers
My Publisher

Lot of love,
Summer
xoxo

Marie watched the way her hand trembled as she clasped the cup and frowned. Just a result of the accident, she told herself and put the cup down. Bright morning sunlight gleamed off the sparkling clean objects in her private hospital room and made everything surreal, and for a second, it felt like time crawled by as she moved her eyes around the room.

"Good morning, lovely lady. How are you feeling?" Tara, Marie's morning nurse, asked as she walked into the room with a smile on her face. The nurse was young, blond, pretty, and dressed in a salmon pink uniform. They all wore that color in this ward, even the male nurses.

"I'm alright, Tara. How are you?" Marie pushed her breakfast tray away and prepared herself for the examination that the nurse would perform. She held her arms out to the side so the nurse could lift her gown and examine her body. The wound was healing but it still stung when the nurse pulled up the bandages to inspect it.

"At least you didn't get an infection, you were lucky," Tara said as she inspected the incision the surgeon made when he opened Marie up to remove the bullet and repair the section of her intestine that was damaged by the bullet.

"I certainly was. Do I get to go home today?" It was a question she'd asked every day for the last month. She was more than ready to go home.

"You do indeed. Your husband is coming to pick you up and the doctor will be here to discharge you shortly." Tara's smile broadened as Marie sighed with relief.

"Thank goodness." Marie let her head fall back to the pillow and smiled for the first time in days. She'd felt so cooped up in here, smothered, and she wanted to be back out in the world again.

"I love you too," Tara said playfully, and Marie laughed.

"Sorry, I didn't mean it like that." Her cheeks felt warm and she put her hands up to hide the blush.

"No offense taken, sweetie. We love it when our patients get to go home." Tara patted Marie's hand and took down her vitals. "I'll remove your IV when the doctor gives me the go-ahead and we'll get you ready to go, alright?"

"Thanks," Marie answered and looked up when the door opened. Matteo was there and her smile grew even brighter as her excitement grew. "I get to go home today."

He wore another one of his tailored

suits, this one a gray that matched his eyes. The suit couldn't hide the fact that her husband was a very healthy male and kept his body in top shape. Her gaze drifted up and down his body before it came back up to his face. She stopped there as he started to answer.

"I know. I have the room prepared for you with everything you might need in place. How are you feeling?" His smile made his fierce gaze softer as he looked from the nurse to Marie. His face always went soft when he looked at her, even if he'd just been glaring at someone for invading his space. And as far as Matteo was concerned, she thought, she was all his space.

That made her blush deeper, and she looked away before she smiled again and looked back.

"I'm good. A little sore, but that's to be expected." She examined his face for signs of trouble, but those glittering gray eyes of

4

his distracted her and nearly took her breath away.

"It is, and it will go soon." Matteo watched as the nurse left them before he came to sit in the chair at the side of her bed. "You'll be back to normal in no time, don't you worry, Marie."

"I'm not. I know I have you." She held her hand out for his and when he took it, she felt a peace come over her. That always happened, every time he touched her, he brought her peace. "I can't wait to get out of here and sleep with you at my side each night."

"Ah. For now, I've decided to put you in your own room, until that wound has healed fully. But I'll come in with you until you get to sleep each night."

"That's your final word on the matter?" She looked up from under her eyelashes as she added a bit of flirtation to her voice.

His left eyebrow crooked before a smile spread over his face. "Of course, it is, dear."

"I see." She pouted for a moment, but

couldn't keep it up. "If that's how it has to be then so be it."

"Only for a little while. I've also hired security for the place. You won't be alone when I have to go out, and there will be men outside at all times."

"I still think they mistook me for someone else," she interrupted, her worry now evident in the way she clutched at his hand. "I don't think it's necessary to go overboard, Matteo."

"I don't know, Marie. There's a lot I still don't know about how this happened, and until I do, you won't be alone or unguarded. That's how it's going to be." His tone told her there was no point to argue so she pursed her lips and nodded.

"Fine. But I won't like it." She glared at him but the minute her eyes caught his, the glare faded. "Especially since it's August and the leaves will start changing soon. That's one of my favorite things to see. Nope, I won't like it at all."

"You don't have to. It'll make me feel better, so that's all that matters."

"Selfish," she spat out and looked away. But her lips twitched. "But in this case, I guess it's good you are."

"I know it is." He patted her hand and they both looked up as the doctor came in.

"Guess who's going home today?" The man's smile was infectious as he came into the room.

Time to go home, at last.

"It's been a month since I was released from the hospital, he still won't let me leave the penthouse. It's almost October. The leaves have changed and I probably won't get to see them now. Our anniversary is soon too." Marie turned to fill Trina's cup with fresh coffee from the French press that she'd brought into the living room. There was regret on her face mixed with a sadness that pulled at the corners of her mouth.

"It's not safe out there," Trina responded, repeating her cousin's own line back to his wife. She couldn't meet Marie's gaze and stared out of the glass panes to the gray, rainy scene outside instead.

"I hate you both, you know that right?" Marie's glare wasn't mean and disappeared quickly. "I just feel like I'm a prisoner all over again."

"What do you mean?" Trina sat forward her head tilted to the right as she leaned in towards Marie.

"Well, I told you about my mother, how ill she was? Well, that prison she had me in was a prison my entire life. Before she developed Parkinson's she was, uh, well, she was an alcoholic." Marie blurted out the words she'd kept hidden away from Trina.

She hadn't wanted to open up that much to the other young woman, hadn't wanted to reveal that embarrassing bit of information, but knew she couldn't hide it anymore. She also knew by now that Trina wouldn't judge her for her mother. Matteo's cousin didn't work like that, unlike the women back home in Louisiana. Trina's acceptance and the love she offered from the first moment they met told Marie she had a real friend, at last.

"When I was growing up, my mother hated me, hated that I existed. No, let me finish..." Marie paused to put her hand out, to implore Trina not to interrupt. She took a breath, pulled at the cuffs of the white long-sleeve t-shirt she wore to ward off the chill in the air. "She wasn't like most women that ended up with a child they hadn't planned to have and learned to make do, or grew to love the child before it was even born. She hated me and she was very open about it."

"That's awful, Marie. I'm so sorry you had a mother like that." Trina sat at the end of the black leather couch and Marie could see she was thinking, but Trina didn't say about what. It was a comfort to Marie that Trina didn't try to reach out to her or try to insist Marie's mother must have loved her.

She just tried to think of how to respond, she was real about it all, and that mattered to Marie. Marie took over the conversation again.

"Oh, I'm still confused about it. I had started to see a counselor before the, um, accident." She swallowed and took another calming breath as she tried to gloss over her stumble, tried to force those memories of the attack on her away. "It was hard. I was the mother more often than not because she was always drunk. I don't know how we paid for things after she spent all her money from acting. I made do, though, and learned to cook. I'd walk down to the grocery store on Saturdays, before I could drive, with a little red wagon, you know the kinds little kids get?" When Trina nodded Marie continued. "I'd take our EBT card in and buy what I could, then I'd go home and make something. I eventually learned to cook something decent."

Marie paused, thought about all the things she wanted to say, all the things that had happened, but it would take too long to go over it all. Trina didn't deserve to have all of that dumped on her, not all of it.

"Anyway, Momma spent more time drunk than sober, but she'd manage to get us to the welfare office every time we had to go, and she'd make sure I was clean and clothed, which meant I'd made sure of it. Probably should have gone in dirty and nasty so they'd take me away, but she was all I had you know? And for all the hell she put me through, she was my mother. I was all she had too."

"That sounds so rough, Marie." Trina took her hand and squeezed it, her eyes full of tears. "I had such a good childhood, so much privilege. Damn, I'm going to cry my makeup off."

"Don't do that, Trina. I just mainly wanted you to understand, you know? Matteo keeping me in the apartment is like that prison all over again. I haven't left the place since we came home from the hospital. It's driving me crazy." She pushed her hands through her hair and pulled at it a little until the sting of it made her stop.

"He loves you though, I can see it. And I can see why now. You're a fighter and one tough little cookie." Trina wiped at tears that had pooled under her eyes and smiled. "You overcome, and that's what he loves."

"Oh, I sometimes think he loves the waif, the poor little woman that needs a savior more than he loves the actual me." She all but whispered the words, but Trina heard.

"I think all men do that, honey. They need to feel like protectors, providers, but I also see how much he admires you, how proud he is of you. You might not see it, but I do. He loves you, even if he hasn't said it."

Marie's eyes went wide, she hadn't told Trina they still hadn't spoken those words. How had she guessed?

"Aunt Celeste wasn't the kind to give affection or allow it. She raised Matteo to be almost a robot. I hate her for it. So, does he.

But I think, maybe, that's part of what draws him to you. You both know that loveless world. You both know the need for that love."

"Oh." Marie could only blink as the truth of Trina's words sank in. "I see."

"We're a pair." Trina laughed and sank back against the couch again. "I can't find love and you can't say it."

"I can't," Marie laughed with Trina, despite the pain hiding in her heart. "But I feel it and I want to say it, but, I just can't. Not unless he does. I can just picture him now, running as far away as possible if I ever said those words to him."

"But maybe he needs to hear them, Marie, before he can say them himself." Trina's gray eyes, so different from Matteo's gray that Marie loved so much, were troubled now. "Maybe you'll have to take yourself out of this prison you've both put each other in."

"Wow, that's deep." Marie was the one that sat back this time, her mind in a whirl all over again. "But I think you might be right."

"Think about it, honey. I have to get going before that thug at the door throws me out for being here too long and tiring you out." Trina leaned over to kiss Marie's cheek then waited until Marie had done the same to her. "I'll be by tomorrow. Maybe you'll be out of prison by then?"

"I hope so. And thanks, for letting me dump all of that on you." Marie followed Trina out and waited at the door until she disappeared behind the elevator doors.

She went back into the living room and sipped at her coffee.

She'd learned one thing from being shot, life was too precious to be caged up, mentally or physically, and right now she was caged up in both ways. She'd have to talk to Matteo this evening and find a way to get him to see that she needed to be able to go out. She'd even agree to have the bodyguards tag along if that's what it took.

He could be a hard man to love, his not

wanting her to go out made it even harder. But she did love him, despite the distance he sometimes put between them, even though he had never said those words to her. He was kind, gentle, fun, and loving with her and she knew that she meant *something* to him.

But she couldn't let that keep her in any kind of prison anymore. If he wanted a wife that could be his match, that could be what he needed, then she'd have to show him that she could be. The only problem was, she wasn't sure how to go about that.

## 2

Matteo rolled over in bed and turned off his alarm clock before it was set to go off. He only set it out of habit now, and just in case he happened to oversleep. His body was trained after all his years of waking up at 6 am and it was rare that he didn't wake up before the alarm went off. Instead of getting up, he turned to look at his wife.

That word still surprised him even though they'd been married for quite a few months now. He knew he'd asked her to be his wife, and knew his logic behind it. To save her from bankruptcy and his Aunt

Celeste's wrath, he'd offered her marriage. He hadn't necessarily planned that marriage to be forever but from the moment she'd looked up into his eyes and said, "I do", she'd become a part of him that he knew he could never let go of. She was his wife. His.

He'd almost lost her, but she was there, safe and sound, and that's where she'd stay. Whether she liked it or not.

He'd like nothing more than to stay home with her, to caress every inch of her body, over and over again, but he had things to do.

After a quick shower, a bite to eat, and getting dressed, Matteo left the penthouse apartment and drove out to the family's construction office. That was where he was supposed to meet Anton, his right-hand man. He walked into the office 45 minutes after he turned the alarm clock off that morning and went straight to his office.

"Come on in, Anton." He waved at the man that sat in a chair in the reception area as he took off his suit coat and put it on the coat rack. "Talk to me."

"Turns out that intel you got was true. It was the de Silvas that attempted to carry out the hit on your wife." Anton looked Matteo square in the eye and Matteo knew that meant that it was best not to ask the big man with the cold, light-green eyes and hard jaw, how he'd attained that information. The whole idea of using Anton to carry out his orders was to keep his name out of the police department's files.

"So, she's out of danger now. Good." Matteo took his seat behind the desk and pushed invoices and purchase orders out of his way. He pulled a laptop from his brief-case and put it in the empty space he'd made. "Or is she?"

Anton hadn't answered him as quickly as he should, and Matteo understood that hesitation. "Find out who ordered the hit then, if it wasn't the de Silvas or the sena-tor's nephew. Or the senator. Fuck, we have too many enemies."

The family had a lot of enemies, a lot of rivals, and it could have also been any number of organizations. Or people. Matteo had a suspicion, but it wasn't one he wanted to fully acknowledge, not yet.

"Yes, boss. Will do." Anton tapped the top of Matteo's desk as a goodbye and left the office. He had a job to do and Matteo knew he'd get it done, no matter the cost.

Matteo knew he had a new problem; one he hadn't quite counted on back when he'd made the decision to marry Marie. His enemies and rivals now knew he had a weakness: his wife. They would use that weakness as much as they could to take him down.

If he'd married her simply to save her from Celeste, he might not care, not much anyway. But he'd come to need her, to need the reassurance of her smile, the warmth that her smile gave him, and the happiness that the sound of her voice brought him. He needed the friendship she gave him and the care that he'd never had from anyone before.

His phone buzzed beside his laptop and he picked it up. "What do you want, Trina?"

"Are you going to keep her locked up forever?" His cousin's impatient voice bombarded his ear and he pulled the phone away from his head and turned on the speaker. He was alone in the office, so it wasn't a problem.

"Why do you have to be so fucking loud, Trina?"

"Because I'm a New Yorker, dumbfuck. Why the hell you think I'm so loud? Now, are you going to keep your wife a prisoner forever or not? Because I'd like to go out to lunch with her today if you don't mind."

"Not gonna happen, Trina. Sorry, but she stays put."

"I hate you right now, do you know that?" She huffed for a long moment and swore under her breath. "Look, I know you're caught up in the throes of your first time of being in love, but you can't smother

her like this, you'll just drive her away. You have to let her out of that apartment soon or she'll lose her mind, Matteo!"

"She'll be fine, and you can visit her whenever you like, you know that." He looked at one of the purchase orders on the pile he'd made and narrowed his eyes. That was far too much lumber, what the fuck were his builders doing on that project?

"You aren't even listening to me now, are you?" She didn't sound happy, and he knew she'd make him pay for it somehow, but right now, he didn't care.

"Gotta go, Trin, talk to you later." He ended the call and went about looking through the recent purchase orders.

That bastard running his work crew was trying to make a little money on the side it looked like. As soon as Penelope, the receptionist/accountant came in, he'd have a talk with her about the foreman. Then he might have to call Anton back in for a new job.

Greedy bastard, he thought as he waited for his laptop to load.

He turned on his VPN, the best money could buy, and looked at the file on a site on the dark web that Anton left for him. The takedown of the de Silvas had been brutal, from what he could see in the pictures, but it had to be. The world had to know you didn't fuck with Matteo or his family. Even if Matteo couldn't be traced back to that takedown.

Trina started to text him then. One every five minutes. Finally, he called her back.

"Stop, will you?" He scrubbed at his smooth jaw with a frustrated hand and sighed. "If she's at home, I control the situation, I control who goes in and who comes out. My men keep her safe. If she's out with you, anyone can attack her. I can't have that."

"Fuck me. Why can't you just say you love her then, Matteo? Why keep her in the dark on that?"

"Because I don't." He said it gruffly,

without conviction, because he knew it was a lie.

"Fucking liar. You do and you can't handle it. That's why you've suddenly become Bluebeard with his wife locked away from the world. Just try not to kill her or cause her to kill herself by keeping her locked away for fuck's sake."

"That's just a little bit rude, Trina." Matteo frowned and glared at the wall. "Am I going to have to cut off your allowance for a month?"

"Do it, see if I care." Trina accepted his dare and spit it back at him. Damn.

"Seriously?" Matteo could think of a dozen other ways to get Trina off his back but knew she was right. Deep down, he knew she was.

"Seriously, Matteo. You need to tell your wife you love her and get her away from here. If she can't walk freely around New York, maybe you should take her somewhere else, where she's fucking safe."

"Now that would be a perfect idea if I

didn't have to be here. But, you know I have to be in New York, I can't leave the family business to anybody else. Not when she's only just given me the reins."

They both knew he was talking about Celeste.

"It's not even really our family business, Matteo. Technically, it's Marie's isn't it?"

"Ah. Yes, I suppose it is." He'd known that they'd even talked about it, but to hear Trina say it out loud really brought the words to life.

"But, you can't give up the baby you were trained your whole life to take over, can you?" Trina sighed loudly and clicked her tongue. "I don't think this is going to end well for you, Matteo, not at the rate you're going."

"That's a chance I'll have to take, Trina. She's worth it." It was all a little confusing, this being in love after the life he'd lived. The things he'd been trained not to need.

"She is. Look, I know you're doing your best, but you have to let her out, soon, Matteo. She can't go on like this too much longer."

"Yeah, yeah, go put your face on or something, Trina. I got shit to do." Matteo hung up before she could interrupt him again.

Damn women, always on his ass. Except Marie wasn't. She had promised him she would be a good little wife, and she had been. She'd done everything he'd ever asked of her and it was unfortunate that he had to pay that obedience back with what amounted to imprisonment. That was the way it had to be until he figured out who had put the hit out on her. Then she could leave.

He thought over what Trina had said about going somewhere, about leaving New York. It might come to that at some point, but he didn't think it had gone that far yet. Not yet.

"I'm here," Penelope, the 58-year-old Jill of all trades, that didn't ask too many questions and knew how to do as she was told, called as she walked into the building. She had iron-gray hair and skin so sun-damaged she looked far older than her 58 years, but she did her job. That was all that mattered.

"Good. I need you to go over the purchase orders that Leon's been putting in for the last few months, see if you find any discrepancies."

"You think he's buying too much and selling it off on his own?" Penelope sat at her desk and turned the desktop computer on. With a slight turn and a flick of her wrist, she turned on the office coffee pot on a table behind her. Penelope was all about efficiency.

"Maybe." Matteo stared at her for a moment and wondered how something like that could get by her. She was the accountant here after all. She didn't seem worried though like she would be if she was in on it. There was nothing about her movements that betrayed any kind of guilt and Matteo knew that she was probably innocent.

Penelope was an accountant, not a project manager or planner. She'd have no clue how much material would be needed. "Look for large increases in supplies, you know, where they were buying three boxes of nails, they started buying 20. Anything like that."

"Will do, Matteo."

Penelope got on with her morning routine, and Matteo soon left to take care of other business elsewhere. He was supposed to have gone down to Louisiana in February to open his casino down there, but he hadn't gone, because he wouldn't leave Marie. He'd sent a representative from the family down in his place. He'd put off going back down there because he hadn't wanted to take Marie back. He didn't think it would be good for her, so he'd delayed the visit. He'd kept telling himself he would go down, but he hadn't made it and now he wouldn't leave her at all. Even if the contract on his wife was finally taken care of, he knew he wouldn't want to leave her. Would it ever truly be over, he wondered as he watched the buildings pass as he drove through the city. This need to be near her, to protect her, from him and the life he lived? The bad that came along with living the good life.

He had a feeling it wouldn't be.

The alert came on through his sound-system that he had a call and he hit a button on the console. "Hi baby, what are you up to?"

"Nothing, honey, just making breakfast." Marie's voice filled the interior of the car and he smiled automatically, totally un-aware that he had. Her voice just made him happy.

"Do you need anything?" he asked, curious about why she'd called.

"No, just wanted to hear your voice. I did wonder something, though."

"What's that?" He'd picked up on the ir-ritated note in her voice and wondered if this would be their first fight.

"Do you want me naked when you get home or dressed? Because I really, really need you." Her voice, always sultry with that southern twang was even more alluring over the phone. His body responded instantly, and he pressed down hard on the gas pedal without meaning to. He eased the pressure of his foot as he regained control and chuckled.

"Why don't you meet me at the door completely naked, Marie, and I'll fuck you right there against the door?"

"Mm, that sounds lovely." She purred down the line and gave a soft laugh of her own. "Or you could meet me in the living room so you can fuck me against the glass again."

"Oh, you know I love that." And he did, he loved fucking her there where he made his claim on her for all to see, although he doubted anyone could see them that high up.

"I do, indeed. So that's a yes on nudity, gotcha." She sighed before she continued. "Where are you going now?"

"I'm going to meet Anton for a late

breakfast, then back to the construction office." He didn't like to lie to her, but she didn't need to know he was going to make sure the shipment they were sending down to New Orleans was in order. Or what was in that shipment.

"That sounds nice. It's fresh air anyway." She sounded wistful, and he knew she wanted to plead with him to let her go out, but she wouldn't. She had too much pride for that.

"It is. Look, I'll bring something home for dinner, so don't worry about that. You just be nice and ready for me when I get there, alright? I'll send you a text when I'm in the parking garage."

"Sounds good. Have a good day." She forced a cheerful note into her voice, and it tore at his heart. She did need to get out at some point.

But not right now.

# 3

Two weeks later, Matteo came home to find Marie still in the bathrobe she'd worn that morning when she'd seen him off to work. That concerned him, was she getting depressed? Her bright smile chased that thought away and he went to sit on the couch with her.

She leaned over to kiss him and say hello. "How are you, darling?"

"I'm good now that I'm home." He stroked her cheek before she pulled away to look at the screen of her laptop.

"I've bought a few more books and

today I watched an entire series about these women that go crazy and get involved in some kind of money laundering scheme with this gangster guy. It was funny." She pushed clean, shiny hair behind her shoulder and sat back, her feet tucked under her. "I can order anything I want on-line, it would seem. All I have to do is wait for it to arrive and the guards bring it to me. After they've inspected it, of course."

"Of course." Her smile was still in place but there was a brittleness to it that both-ered him.

"It's perfect really, I can even order gro-ceries online. I never have to leave this per-fect, safe place." Her eyes turned to his then, their deep brown so unlike anything he'd ever seen before. It made him ache now, to see that hint of pain in those eyes. The per-fect bird, in the perfect cage.

That was the accusation in her eyes, at least.

"I'm glad you're finding ways to stay busy."

"I've got the treadmill over there for when I need to walk," she waved at the treadmill in the corner of the living room, "I have the phone if I want to talk to someone. And books and movies at my fingertips. Oh, and the doctor has agreed to make house visits, as has the counselor."

"Good." He nodded but he wasn't sure if he wanted the counselor coming here. The doctor might be needed at some point, but the counselor? It might take some explaining to stop any questions they had about why Marie wasn't allowed to leave the place.

"Trina came over for lunch, and she's coming back tomorrow." Marie slid down on the couch, her eyes on the darkness outside the glass wall. "I wish one of the windows would open."

"What good would climate control be then?" he responded, guilt niggling at him. He knew what she meant, even if she didn't say it. She wanted fresh air.

"You're right. Shall we have dinner?" She

got up from the couch and walked down to the kitchen.

He wondered if she'd been on the treadmill at all today, or if she'd put on clothes when Trina came over or if she'd stayed in her robe. He wanted to ask, but he didn't want to make her feel self-conscious. He wanted to know if she was showing signs of depression, though. He decided to text Trina.

Trina texted back promptly and told him to fuck off and ask Marie herself. Damn.

"What are we having?"

"Well, since I have so much time on my hands, I made a beef roast, homemade macaroni and cheese, au gratin potatoes, and steamed some vegetables." She threw the response over her shoulder as she took the roast out of the oven where it had been resting and then pulled plates down from the cabinet. "Do you want horseradish with the roast?"

"I think so, yes." He got it from the

fridge and took that and a bottle of wine to the table. She'd already put two glasses and the tableware down.

"Alright, let's eat." She smiled as she set a perfectly portioned plate down in front of him and one at the place where she sat. "How was your day?"

He gave her the usual answer, that it was fine and there'd been no problems. He left out the part about discovering the foreman of his construction crew had been stealing from him, and the fact that Anton had burned the guy's house down for it. It was better than killing him and the man got the message and left town with his girlfriend. A very good idea.

"How's your roast?" she asked after a while.

It was the most boring conversation they'd ever had and he knew it was his own fault. He'd done this to her, made her his prisoner, because of his own fears. He just didn't know what to do about it. Instead, he decided to distract her the best way he knew how.

"It's not as good as licking the taste of you from your skin, Marie. But it's close." He grinned over at her and she gave him a saucy wink.

"You'd better save that for after dessert. I made cherry cheesecake." She took a bite of macaroni and cheese into her mouth while she watched his eyes go wide in excitement.

"Now you know that's my favorite." He saw the way her nostrils flared and knew where this was headed.

"I do. But is it as good as my skin?" Her lips twitched in a way he couldn't take his eyes off of, even though her eyes beckoned.

"I think we should find out how good it is on your skin."

That was all he had to say as they both got up, took their plates into the kitchen, and brought back the cheesecake in a glass dish. Marie cut a portion of it for him, but rather than eat it with his spoon, he directed her to sit in front of him on the table.

Her robe gaped open to reveal she only had on a pair of pink cotton panties. He liked those he decided as he spread some of the dessert down her smooth thighs. Slowly, with great care, he licked up each morsel of the cherries, sauce, and cheesecake on her thighs. By the time he cleaned off the other leg, she could barely breathe, and her eyes were a warm shade of brown that he only saw when she was aroused.

"Let's get these off, baby." He pulled the panties down and threw them behind his chair once they were free of her legs. "Now, to taste the real delicacy in this house."

He set her feet to rest on each side of the armrests and leaned forward to inhale her clean scent. Marie leaned back on the table, propped up on her elbows as he stroked her with the very tips of his fingers. Not an invasive touch, for now, he was only exploring her, letting her build to something more.

"You are a beautiful woman, Marie, but to me, you're everything I could have ever wanted." He spoke the words so softly he doubted she even heard him. He worked his hands under her to tilt her hips up when she didn't say anything in response and ran his tongue deep into her folds. That got a very quick response.

A glass crashed to the floor as she moaned loudly somewhere above him. She must have reached out to hold onto the edge of the table and knocked the glass off. Good, she was already halfway to mindlessness then.

He practiced everything he'd learned she liked over the months and used every one of those skills expertly as he sensually explored her with his tongue, his teeth, and his lips. When her hips started to rotate, he pulled away and stood over her. He pressed his hips into hers so she could feel how hard he was, grinding himself into her until it was a torture he couldn't bear any more.

He eased off of her center to explore her breasts. They were firm and full, the tips a dusky rose that beckoned to be kissed.

Again, Matteo teased her expertly, with a twist of his fingers and the suction of his lips, he aroused his wife into a state where her legs wrapped around his hips to grind up into him, not caring that they were both on the kitchen table, or that they had a bed to do this in. She just wanted him. And when she begged him for the release she needed, he pulled away and picked her up.

With careful steps, he took her into their bedroom and put her down on the bed. He stood at the foot of the bed ready to climb over her, but she had other ideas. She turned over and stood up, just to bend right back down. His grin was full of cocky pleasure as he rubbed a large hand over the mound of her ass.

"Is that how you want it, Marie? You want me to take you from behind? To make you mine? To make you scream my name?"

"I do, Matteo, please, don't make me wait." She twisted her hips and pushed back into him, the robe now in a puddle in the hallway somewhere. He ran a finger down her perfect spine, over the curve of her hip, before he placed both hands firmly on each side of her hips in a way that made her suck in a breath in anticipation, only to pull her back into his erection.

"Fuck," she screeched angrily. "You still have your clothes on, Matteo?"

"Patience, my lovely. You have to be patient." He ground his hard length into her, just to tease her, but it made the ache there worse. He was punishing himself now, not just her.

He wanted her desperately, wanted to be inside of those slick walls of hers, to lose himself in her, but he wanted this to last, he wanted her to be completely in a mess before he let himself go.

He pulled his right hand from her hips, slid it down the crevice of her ass, to slide down into her silky folds to find her clit. "That's what you need, right, darling? You need to get off. That's all you need."

He knew it wasn't, but he loved the way he could make her come fast and hard with his fingers. It was a slower process when he used his mouth on her, but with his fingers? It took seconds and she was moaning and twitching uncontrollably. He watched her back arch now, watched the way she pushed her pussy out towards him, and knew that the second her back relaxed he'd be inside her.

He pushed his zipper down, undid his belt, and pulled his other hand away from her just as her back relaxed. With a firm grip, he guided himself to her entrance and paused to put his hand back on her hip. She couldn't wait though and pushed herself down onto him with an audible sigh of relief.

"That's what I wanted Matteo. I wanted your cock, baby. I wanted you inside of me." She'd learned to talk to him the way he liked. She'd learned to tell him what she liked, what she wanted, to use her words to arouse him the same as he did with her.

"Fuck," he ground out as her little ploy nearly undid him. The sensation of the soft slickness around his throbbing cock was almost too much, but he caught himself, even when she began to bounce on him. With a growl, he tensed his fingers on her hips. "Sit still, woman."

"Only if you promise to fuck me hard?" She looked back at him over her right shoulder, a gleam in her eyes. She'd paused, long enough for him to catch his breath and his arousal. Thank goodness.

"Baby, you'd better hang onto something, because, yes, I'm going to fuck you very, very hard."

She laughed as he began to give her exactly what she'd asked for. Hard, fast, he thrust himself into her over and over, until he felt her spasm around him, until she croaked out his name on a strangled sob of pleasure.

He could feel how hard she came. He could feel it in the way her pussy gripped at him, milked him, as she strangled out sounds underneath him. Matteo dug his toes into the carpet and held on for all he was worth, but he couldn't hold back any longer. Not with the way she was going off.

He cried out as his pleasure shot up his spine, straight back down and through his cock. His fingers tensed on her hips, held her tight to his body, as he let himself go at last. The pleasure only lasted a few seconds, if that long, but the build-up to it was exquisite, and that brief, eternal moment seemed to go on forever sometimes, as it did now.

She might only get one fuck out of him tonight. He knew that wasn't true though, he'd find the will somewhere if she wanted another round. He always did. Not just to please her, though, but because he couldn't get enough of her himself.

He crawled up the bed and pulled her into his arms a few moments later, and brushed her hair out of her face. "You alright?"

He could feel she was still trembling, and her right hand shook a little when she brought it up stroke his cheek. "I'm fine."

Was she though? He watched her and soon the trembles stopped and she sighed happily. He watched her fingers and saw her pinky twitch a couple of times, but then that stopped too. She was alright.

"Can you stand up?" he asked with a laugh because he knew her legs would probably shake when she tried to get up.

"Maybe. Let's try. I want some cranberry juice and maybe some vodka." She laughed when she nearly fell on the floor, but she managed to stand up and walk with him to the kitchen. "I'll have this, then grab a shower. We'll watch a movie after if you want?"

"Sure, but maybe I'll join you in the shower..." he started to say but she shook her head.

"No, you won't, buddy. I need to scrub up and get to bed so my legs will stop shaking. Another round of that tonight and I won't be able to get up tomorrow." She gave him a look with her eyebrow cocked over her eye and he laughed.

With his hands held up, he turned away and opened the fridge to take out a bottle of apple juice. "Fine, fine. If that's how you want to be. Movie and sleep, like old people do."

"Oh, not quite honey. I doubt old people fuck like we just did." She laughed, and it drew his eyes down to her naked breasts. Neither one of them had dressed and he couldn't help but stare at her. Every inch of her was perfect.

"No, I doubt they do," he muttered and pushed her up against the fridge to kiss her deep and long; a slow but soulful kiss that had her clinging to him with renewed hunger. "I hope this fridge doesn't tip over."

They were the last words he said before she pulled his head back down to hers for another kiss.

# 4

Matteo winced the next morning and pulled his sunglasses down as the sunlight hit his eyes. Marie's attention kept him awake far past his bedtime the night before and his eyes watered at the strength of the sun. But the sting didn't dim his smile as he got into his car, not even a little bit.

She might be restless, tired of being cooped up, and on the verge of tearing off the door and running out of the apartment, but she still wanted him. Maybe that was part of the reason she'd been so insatiable the night before, he reasoned as he pulled out into traffic and headed for the construction office. She had to burn off her energy somehow, and obviously, the treadmill wasn't enough.

The smile stayed on his face when he walked through the door and saw how Penelope frowned at him. She stared at him with narrowed eyes as he started to whistle softly and pour out a cup of coffee.

"What's wrong with you?" she finally asked when he waltzed into his office without closing the door as he usually did.

"Not a thing, Penelope. I'm just fine." He looked up as she walked into his office, that smile still front and center.

"Are you sure you aren't sick or something? You're smiling. You don't smile. Not like that, anyway." Her accent wasn't as refined as his, hers was more Bronx, the sound of the public school she'd attended. He was used to it, but he did miss the sweet, slow sound of Marie's accent.

"I'm a man with a wife that keeps him happy, Penelope, is that a bad thing?" It was probably the most he'd ever revealed about himself to her and the shock made both of her eyebrows shoot up her forehead.

"You're sick. I'm going to order you some soup for lunch." She muttered the words as she walked away, taken off guard by his candor.

"I'm fine, really, Penelope," he called out but she didn't answer, she just sat out there muttering about newlyweds and how weird they were.

Matteo chuckled quietly and opened his laptop to begin his day. He had to go down to one of the warehouses to meet Anton after lunch, but for now, he needed to go over the information he'd received about the casino in Louisiana. He had several reports to go through for the other businesses they had up there in New York as well, so when his Skype started to ring, he breathed a sigh of annoyance. There was only one person that called him on Skype.

"Hello, Celeste," he said as he got up to close his office door. When he came back around the desk, he saw her face on the screen.

Her face was in shadow, cast by a large-brimmed hat she wore, her eyes covered with sunglasses as she sipped at a glass of dark red wine. "Hello, Matteo. How are you, my boy?"

"I'm fine. How are you, Aunt?" His voice was crisp and to the point, without any emotion. He always shut down when he talked to her or was anywhere near her. That's how she'd wanted him, emotionless and cold, so that's what he gave her.

"And your little backwater wife? How is she? Knocked her up yet?" She popped an olive into her mouth and Matteo would have wondered where she was if he'd cared.

"No, I haven't, and she's fine." He tried not to grind his jaw, but she made it hard not to. "What do you want, Celeste?"

"I want a lot of things, Matteo, but you defied me when you married that trashy girl. So now, I have to decide on new things to want. Unless you'd be kind enough to divorce the girl? She's not our kind, you know? She's far beneath you. Not at all what I had in mind for you."

"We're Catholics, Aunt, we don't divorce, remember?" Matteo leaned back in his seat, his hands crossed in his lap. If he didn't lean back, he'd hang up on her, and he didn't want to do that. It would show her that she'd got to him and he'd never let her know that.

"There is annulment, Matteo." She spoke the words softly, a sibilant note in her voice that turned into a dangerous hiss. Was she ordering him to annul his marriage?

"That would be a bit hard to do, Celeste. We've consummated the marriage, we were both of age, in our right minds, and whatever else the grounds are for annulment. It's not happening."

"I know a priest here, he'll do as I ask." Her face wavered on the screen but then settled. She was in Italy, so the connection wasn't going to be that good anyway.

"Celeste, drop it." He barked the words out, an order for her to stop her nonsense.

"Oh, now there's the manhood you somehow lost when you married that little bit of trash of yours," she gloated across the miles, and it only irritated Matteo even more.

"If you make one more remark about her, Celeste, one more..." he started but she just laughed a trilling, spiteful laugh, before she looked directly into the camera.

"You'll do what? Run off with her and never speak to me again? I highly doubt that."

"Don't push me. That's all you've done my entire life and I've had my fill of it. You put me in charge here, so I suggest you let me do my job and get on with it, instead of calling me up to insult my wife."

"Oh, like that is it?" She leaned into the camera to look more closely at his face. Her lips pursed in cruel delight as she saw what he couldn't hide from her. "Interesting.

Fine, have your way, Matteo. But take care you don't get burned."

"Goodbye, Celeste." He'd barely finished when she ended the call.

That fucking bitch, he thought as he closed the laptop and sat back in his chair again. But maybe she was right, in a way.

His feelings for Marie made him weak, made them both a target of those that wanted to see him fail, of those that wanted what he had. That was part of the reason he kept her locked behind guards and a very heavy door. He could breathe knowing she was safe at home. If she was outside of those walls, away from the protection of his men, he'd constantly be in panic mode.

No, he had her where he wanted her, safe and secure.

He hated to be weak, and she was very much his weakness now. He needed her in ways he'd never known he could need any-one. The fact that Celeste knew that now infuriated him, but he couldn't do anything about that. And what was that warning at the end, before she closed the call?

He knew she'd hated Marie's mother, Ruby, and with good cause. But Matteo knew something about Celeste that nobody else did: it wasn't that Ruby had been her husband's lover that caused her to hate Ruby, it was that Ruby had caused her embarrassment. And then she'd had the gall to have the child that his late uncle, Nick, hadn't given to her. That's what really infuriated Celeste, that's what had motivated her.

Had that hatred transferred over now to Marie? It would make a sort of convoluted sense. Marie was the child that had caused her further embarrassment, proof that her husband had strayed. Did that deserve Celeste's hatred now? And if it did, was Celeste willing to kill over it?

That thought, finally fully formed in his mind, stunned Matteo. Would Celeste be so cruel, so fucking selfish in her decades-old wallow into self-pity, that she'd order a hit on her nephew's wife? The answer to that came swiftly and without a flicker of hesitation. She would if it got her the vengeance she craved, no matter the cost.

A new idea developed as he looked around the office, a spartan place with only his desk, desk chair, a file cabinet, and a space heater that he used in the winter. Four walls covered in cheap wall panel boards nailed up long before he was born, made the room feel almost... coffin-like. An air conditioner kept the room cool from a window to his left. He pulled at the sapphire blue silk tie he wore and at his collar as thoughts bombarded him.

If it was Celeste, if she'd called the hit, he had nowhere to hide, no safe house that she didn't know about. There was nowhere they could run to for safety.

Just as quickly, his thoughts jumped back to whether Celeste was the threat. Maybe that's what Celeste meant when she told him to be careful and not get burned. He'd have to leave Marie to not be taken down with her? But that would never happen, not as long as he had breath in his body. He'd never leave his wife. She needed him.

He needed her.

With steady hands, he picked up his phone and called Anton. "Scratch whatever you're doing and meet me down at the river warehouse."

Matteo knew he didn't have to elaborate, Anton would know which one he meant.

"Sure, boss. Be there in 10 minutes."

"Good. Come alone," Matteo added, simply because Anton sometimes brought one of the other guys with him.

"Will do."

Matteo left his laptop, but picked up his briefcase, closed and locked the office door, and let Penelope know he was going out. He drove to the warehouse quickly and got there before Anton did. When his man arrived, he got out of the car and they walked together into the silent building. Another empty building, another place for them to hide illicit goods.

"What's up, Matteo?" Anton asked, his light-green eyes lit with curiosity.

"I need you to find me a safe place, a place that nobody, not even the family, can know about." Matteo looked at him, the man he'd chosen because his loyalty was to Matteo, not Celeste. He was the only one that Matteo could trust right now, besides Marie.

"Can do." Anton, always a man that spoke only the necessary words, kept it brief.

"Good. And don't use any devices to tell me where. In-person only. Get me two tickets to wherever it is you're going to send us, rent a house in your name, and I'll make sure you're paid immediately for it. Oh, choose somewhere remote, but with good views for security."

"Yep. Want me to come with?" Anton asked, his dark eyebrows quirked.

"Maybe, I'm not sure yet. Get another

ticket, just in case. Yeah, do that."

"Plane, right?"

"Yeah, it'll be risky, so don't land us near wherever the house is. Have a car there waiting for us. I'll drive to the house."

"Yep." Anton nodded and waited. Matteo watched him and felt relief that he could trust this man at least.

"Get it done and come by this evening. I'll be at home. Like I said, nothing online, no devices used. Go out to the airport and get the tickets if you have to."

"No problem, boss." Anton nodded his understanding.

"Alright. I'm going to get back to Marie. I'll be there all day if you need me."

"Sure, boss. I'll be by as soon as I can. I know a place, a really good place, but it's colder there than it is here. Pack warm."

"Where is this place?"

"An old cop friend of my dad's from Montana has a place out there he uses during the winter for hunting. It'll be perfect for you."

"Anybody know about it?" Matteo wasn't so sure about that, it was too connected to the area.

"No, only him, his family, my dad, and me. That's it."

"Okay. It doesn't sound bad. I always wanted to go out west, anyway. Never did, but always wanted to." Matteo realized he'd picked up Anton's habit of brief speech and shook himself. "Good. Arrange that then."

"Got ya." Anton knew the meeting was over then and said one last thing. "I'll get the keys from the guy, bring them by to you later. When do you want to leave?"

"Tonight, if possible." Matteo didn't want to seem like a scared rabbit, but he had to get Marie away from New York, he knew that deep in his gut.

"Anything's possible, with enough money." Anton gave Matteo a wink and Matteo nodded.

"That I have plenty of. Give him what he wants."

"Yep," Anton said and waved as he

headed off to his car.

Matteo got back in his own car, headed in the direction of home. He didn't think about the fact that the word "home" now conjured up images of Marie, he'd come to accept that. It was as true as the fact that he needed air to breathe - something he couldn't change, so why try?

With his foot on the brake at a red light, Matteo scrolled through the songs listed on the console. He found the one he wanted to listen to and pressed play. The song began that slow thumping bass that he loved as the light changed to green. It was a slow, sensual song about something he thought about often now... getting his woman off.

Tonight, if things panned out, there'd be no sex, but one night off wouldn't hurt them. Not when it meant they would be in peace, that Marie would be in new surroundings where she'd be safe. And it would give Anton time to find out if Celeste had committed the ultimate betrayal and paid someone to murder his wife.

He would seriously lose his shit if he found out she had, but for now, he was trying to keep his cool. There were still quite a few people to consider, quite a few possibilities to cross off his list. But something in his gut told him this threat came from closer to home.

He sent Penelope a message to tell her to keep the office in order on her own for a bit, not a new occurrence, and then drove into the parking garage. As he rode up the elevator to the penthouse, he tried to picture Marie's excitement at leaving the apartment at last and it brought a smile to his face. Her delight always pleased him. And this would truly please her.

From what he knew about Montana, which was next to nothing, he knew there would be little chance that anyone could sneak up on them. With Anton around, as an added pair of eyes, Marie would be safe. And maybe she could even go for walks outside.

# 5

Marie stared at her husband, her face blank, and her breath held. "What?"

"Pack some warm clothes, darling, we're taking a little trip." His eyes watched her face carefully, waiting for something. Even though he'd said it twice now, she didn't believe him.

"No, you haven't let me out of the house since you brought me home from the hospital. I don't believe you're taking me somewhere on a trip now." She sat down on the couch carefully, afraid that any wrong move would, she wasn't sure, break the spell?

Maybe it might make him laugh loudly and call her stupid like the bullies used to do when she was in school and they'd pretend to be her friend long enough to pull some practical joke on her.

Her heart would shrivel up into a dried-out walnut if he did that to her. It had been hard enough to put up with his guard-enforced imprisonment, but to think that now when she'd learned to trust him, to love him, he'd make her the butt of his joke?

She didn't think that was possible. She thought he loved her, but this was a really terrible joke. She looked away from him, out of the glass wall to the light-blue sky that made her feel calm. She took a deep breath, held it, and let it out slowly. "This isn't funny, Matteo, and I really don't appreciate it."

"What?" He stood over her, his hand in his hair before he bent down to kneel in front of her. "Baby, I'm going to take you away from here for a little while. I don't know how long, but you might even be able to take walks there. Get some fresh air. Anton's getting everything sorted and if he can manage it, we're catching a flight today. So, please, go pack some clothes."

He chuckled quietly before he leaned in to kiss her. "I wouldn't be that cruel to you, Marie, never, not in a million years. You mean too much to me."

"Do I?" She felt her heart thud back to life as blood surged through it like a startled bunny rabbit, and tried to catch her breath when he nodded. "You're really taking me out of here?"

That wasn't what she wanted to ask though. She wanted to ask him more about what she really meant to him, wanted to ask him if he cared about her, but knew that it wasn't the time for that. She was almost free of this place.

"Yes, Marie. Now come on, let's get packed. I don't know how much time we have before Anton will be here. He's going with us." That last part was called out over his shoulder as he walked back to their bedroom.

"I don't care if you bring along the entire New York Jets football team, Matteo, we're leaving here." She stood up after him and raced past him to the bedroom. She almost knocked him over she was in such a rush. "Let's get packing."

She had three bags when she got finished, which was far more clothes than she'd had a year ago at the same time. She also had shoes, cosmetics, toiletries, jewelry, and other things that she didn't have before. Matteo had given her all of that, but he'd given her far more, which was why she hadn't called the police and demanded her freedom.

He'd given her love, a reason to live, even if they were both too broken to talk it out, to say it out loud. She'd had enough sessions with her counselor to know that she had trust issues and that she needed more counseling. But she'd also had enough of Matteo's affection, the care he showed to her, to know that even keeping her locked away was a sign of how much he cared about her.

He hadn't said much about his aunt, but Trina had explained quite a lot about the woman that had raised Matteo. She could imagine the life he'd lived. It wasn't any easier for him to show love than it was for her.

"You ready?" he called out as he came out of the shower, a towel knotted low on his hips.

"I am. But, um, that's pretty tempting." She waved at the towel knotted loosely around his hips. "Are you sure we don't have time?"

"I don't know, I told Anton not to con-tact me on any devices. We might." He backed her up against the bed until she couldn't back up anymore and went down.

Matteo moved in between her knees as she wrapped her arms around his waist and stuck her finger into the edge of the towel to pull it apart. The soft black cloth fell to the floor with a quiet sound, but she didn't hear it. She was too busy pressing soft kisses to his lower abdomen and inhaling his scent.

Unfortunately, that was the moment the guard knocked at the door.

"Fuck, Anton's here." Matteo slowly pulled away his eyes sealed to Marie's with heat tempered by regret. "Later, we'll finish this later."

"Oh, we will, baby." Marie grinned and got up to rearrange her clothes. "I'll let him in. You get dressed."

"Thanks."

She walked down to open the door and let the large man into the apartment. "Want a drink?"

"No, thanks, Marie." He shuffled in the doorway, his eyes down on the floor. "Is Matteo home?"

"Yeah, he'll be out in a minute. I hear we're going on an adventure?"

"That we are. You all packed?" His only movement was to shove his hands in his pockets.

Marie grinned when she realized he wasn't the asshole she'd taken him for the few times she'd met him in the past. She'd thought he was gruff to the point of rudeness, but it finally dawned on her that the man was painfully shy around her. She smothered a laugh of delight and stepped back a few more feet.

"Yeah, we're all packed up and ready to go. I can't wait to leave these walls behind and get some fresh air. Where are we going? He told me to pack warm clothes, and it's still warm in most places." She leaned against the wall, nonchalant and careful to try to put the man at ease.

He actually shuffled his foot on the carpet before he looked up quickly, then right back down. "I guess you are ready for some fresh air. About where we're going. It's a place up in Montana. Up in the mountains. It can be pretty cold at night up there, but not so bad during the day. Um..."

He'd stopped to take a deep breath and

Marie figured he was trying to think of something to say. Matteo saved him from having to talk to Marie by coming out of the bedroom with several pieces of their luggage. "Hi, Anton, what do you know?"

"Flight's in two hours, private plane, paid for with cash. I've rented a car, so we'll have transport once we get there."

"Good, good."

Marie didn't really pay much attention after that, she was too busy staring at the door. The door that was about to open and take her to fresh air and freedom. The men didn't waste too much time and Matteo soon ushered her out of the building and down to the car Anton had chosen to drive them to the airport.

She could feel the heat in the parking garage, despite the green maxi dress she wore, so when she got in the car to find it was a bit warm, she cracked the window a fraction of an inch. She held her face up to the tinted window and let the tiny crack of air blow over her hair and face as the air conditioner started to work. It was so good to feel that air, to breathe it in, and Marie felt relief as an almost physical sensation on her skin and in her brain.

Freedom, even if she was in a car. She was free of that penthouse, free of the overwhelming oppression of being locked away again. She remembered not that long ago she'd decided to have it out with Matteo, to demand he take her outside somewhere. She would have to show him she was his match, she'd decided. But between the moment of that decision and the point where he came home, her mind had shut down those thoughts.

She'd spent so much of her life being in someone's prison, first her mother's and then Matteo's, that she'd learned to just deal with the moments as they came along. He hadn't kept her in to control her, that was the difference now, she thought as the car pulled into the airport. He'd kept her in to keep her safe. The thing he didn't seem to understand was that she only felt safe when she was with him.

Even with those guards outside the door, she felt unsafe every moment of the day until Matteo came home. That's when she came back to life. Even when Trina came to visit her, she was still on autopilot, just taking one breath at a time until that moment when he walked through the door.

"Keep your eyes peeled, Anton," she heard Matteo mutter and looked at him more closely as they walked to the jet that waited for them.

"Always, boss," Anton replied.

Marie didn't really pay too much attention to that, though, she was finally looking at her husband and saw that tension drew fine lines around his eyes, and pulled at his lips. He was also hyper-vigilant, with one hand on her elbow as he looked around with every step they took.

She knew he'd been rattled by that attempt on her life, so rattled he'd locked her away. But the police were handling it, surely? That was the moment when she was forced to admit that she might be a little naïve about the world. She'd lived a sheltered life, locked away with her mother. She'd seen movies and television shows that portrayed good cops and bad, and seen the nightly news. So she wasn't completely innocent of the world, but was she putting too much faith in the police?

Matteo wasn't a stupid man, he was quite intelligent, and if he was worried then it was for a reason. She put those thoughts away the moment she stepped onto the plane. White leather seats that looked like they were made from clouds beckoned to her. She'd had a lot of trouble sleeping lately, and she knew they'd be on the plane for a while. Maybe she could catch a nap while they were in the air.

She blamed her injuries from the attack and the lack of sleep for her inability to remember words over the last few weeks. She blamed her inability to sleep on the fact that she'd been attacked. It was a circle of blame that kept her from panic. If she was honest with herself, she'd admit that she recognized those symptoms from her mother's illness. She couldn't do that, though. Not yet. She'd had one scare before the attack, that was enough for now.

"Are you alright, darling?" he asked her an hour later. She'd almost drifted off as the sun went down behind the clouds, but turned her head to face him now.

"I'm great. I'm not stuck at home anymore. And we're going on an adventure." She took his right hand in her left one and brought it to her lips. "Thank you."

"Ah, don't thank me too much. I have a feeling this is going to be nothing but wilderness and trees."

"That's fine, as long as I can go out in it. Can I?" She felt her heart catch while she waited, hoping that he'd say yes.

"Let us check it out, but yeah, I think you can." He gave her a tentative smile, the edges of his lips curled up as if unsure he should smile at that point.

"Oh, that will be wonderful." She sighed happily as her heart began to beat normally again. "I can't wait."

Anton snored softly behind her and she giggled quietly enough that it wouldn't wake him.

"Does he have a partner?" she asked Matteo in a whisper, her face close to his ear.

"Anton? I don't know. You mean a significant other, right?" He turned his head to ask.

"Yeah, does he have a girlfriend? Or a boyfriend? I'm assuming he's not married, he doesn't have a ring on."

"Not that I know of. Either one. But, we don't have those kinds of talks. Maybe he does? I don't know. Why?" His eyes narrowed with playful suspicion. "Do I have a reason to be worried?"

"Not at all. I just know someone that might be perfect for him."

"Oh, fuck no. Don't go playing matchmaker." He laughed to smooth over the harshness of his words. "Besides, the only person you know to fix him up with is Trina, and she'd eat him for breakfast."

"You think so?" She tilted her head to the side quizzically, her eyes amused. "I have a feeling she'd bring out exactly what she wanted to in him."

"Maybe, but I don't need my cousin dating my employee. That could get awkward."

"Perhaps so." She tilted her head back now, looking at him with amusement. "We'll see."

"Oh, brother." He slid down in his seat and closed his eyes. "You're a handful, do you know that?"

"I know something you can fill your hands with if that's what you mean." She whispered it directly into his ear, delighted at the way the silky skin of his earlobe tickled her lips. "And a few other things too."

"Mm, I know you do." He shifted around in his seat again, but this time she could tell it was to ease the way his pants stretched over his hips. Had that aroused him?

She was fascinated with the way he responded to her, even now, after they'd been together so long. All she had to do was whisper to him and he would respond as if she'd just done a strip show for only him, the best strip show ever performed. She loved that small amount of power she had over him.

She'd never had power over anyone before, not in any way, not really. She probably did over her mother, after she'd become bedridden, but even then, her mother was the one in control. Now, though, she knew that she could distract her husband, could get his attention, by doing nothing more than leaning forward to let him see her cleavage in a low-cut top, or by whispering in his ear. The brush of her fingers against the inside of his wrist would do it too, she'd noticed.

There were dozens of ways she could distract him and she did it often. Not just because it was a display of her power, but because she reacted the same way to him. It was an equal power share in a funny sort of way, she decided.

"Do you think we'll make it to this secret house in the middle of nowhere before we have to find some privacy?" she asked him as another tease.

"If you keep it up, I'll take you to that tiny bathroom, turn you to face the wall, and fuck you until you can't stand up. Or is that what you're after?"

She looked up into gray eyes that had turned a dark shade of steel, a sure sign that he was close to letting her have her way.

"Maybe it is." The quirk of her lips was his undoing and she giggled as he pulled her up from her seat to take her to the back of the plane. Sometimes it was the little things that gave you the most pleasure, she decided, just before he turned her to face the wall and slid his hands up beneath her dress.

# 6

Matteo stirred onions that were almost caramelized as Marie came into the kitchen, her face soft from sleep. He turned and took her face into his hands, kissed her lips gently, and pulled away to look down at her.

"The smell wake you up?" he asked with another peck on her cheek before he turned back to the onions.

"What? No, I just woke up," she scrubbed at her face and looked at the onions in the pan with a confused look. "Why can't I smell the onions?"

"Pardon?" He turned his head back to her as she poured a glass of water at the sink on the other side of the counter.

"I can't smell the onions." She leaned back against the white marble counter of their new, temporary home, and sniffed as if to clear her nostrils. "I don't have a cold, my nose isn't stopped up, but I can't smell anything."

"Hm, that's odd. Maybe it's from the flight?" He thought about it for a minute and continued. "Maybe that's plugged up your sinuses, but you just can't feel it."

"Maybe." A smile replaced the frown she'd worn, and she moved to wrap her arm around his waist. "What's for dinner?"

"A very simple curry in a jar, along with the pasta. I got them from that little store we stopped at in town. Not much, but it'll fill us up and be warm." He nodded at the table behind him. "Want to keep me company?"

"Sure. Where's Anton?" She sat down in one of the simple pine chairs that matched the table. It was a large house with two floors, three if you counted the attic. Anton had taken up residence at the highest point and had spent the hour that Marie napped carrying up split wood for a small box-stove that would provide warmth up there.

"He's having a look around the property, checking the fences. He'll be back before dinner is finished."

"Alright. Isn't it strange how much colder it is out here?" She pulled at the cuffs of her flannel pajama shirt, her eyes searching for a heat source.

"I guess it's the elevation," he said as he put cubed chicken into the pan with the onions. "I'm not sure I'd like it getting cold so soon, it's not even October until next week. But it seems a nice place."

The house was a very fancy log cabin, but still a log cabin. The décor was rustic, male-oriented with a lot of hardwoods and dark browns and reds. Everything from the dark brown leather couch to the Navajo rugs on the floors, to the many deer heads on the walls, screamed a man had designed the place.

The first floor was made up of a large living room with a glass wall, a bathroom, one bedroom, a study, and a kitchen. Upstairs were four more bedrooms, two bathrooms, and above that was the attic. That section was designed like an open-spaced apartment, with its own bathroom and a kitchenette that split the living room and bedroom into separate but still open spaces. The only heat came from the two fireplaces downstairs, one in each bedroom upstairs, and the one in the attic. That accounted for the massive pile of chopped and split wood outside.

"Okay, I'm going to have a shower, see if that will clear my head before I eat. That nap you suggested was a good idea."

"I know you haven't been sleeping well, so I thought it might. Hopefully, with all of this fresh air and freedom, you'll be able to sleep better." Matteo pulled his bottom lip in between his teeth and frowned. He didn't like mentioning the fact that he'd basically held her prisoner for weeks now.

"See you in a bit." She kissed him on the cheek on the way out.

Matteo watched her go, concerned that she hadn't been able to smell the onions. She should have been able to smell them, but as he'd said, maybe it was the flight, and being somewhere new at such a higher elevation than she was used to. Or something like that.

They were about five miles outside of Thompson Falls, Montana, up the side of a mountain covered in snow. A couple of thousand feet above sea level, at least. In Louisiana, she'd been near to, maybe even below sea level. In New York, they were a few dozen feet above sea level. Here, they were all but in the clouds, in comparison to the other places she'd lived. Maybe that's all it was, no need to worry.

He'd done his research when she'd first mentioned going to the doctor. He'd read about the signs and symptoms of Parkin-

son's Disease. He was worried, but the like-
lihood that she'd develop the disease was
very slim. Everything he'd read said the disease wasn't inherited, in most cases. It was
the "most cases" that bothered him.

He knew that if she developed it, he
would be there to take care of her, to provide her with the best doctors and treatments that money could buy. But how
would she deal with it? With him there,
hopefully, she'd cope.

He sighed deeply as he listened for the
sounds of her moving around upstairs.
She'd just come out of the shower, so she'd
be down soon. He had found a way to hide
his worry, to rein it in. He was set to be the
next big Mafia king, the one with all the
power and control. He couldn't be seen to
be weak, even with his wife.

Even if he wanted to be with his wife.

She came in just as he put the pasta into
a pot of boiling water, Anton not far behind
her. This was weird, having Anton around
so much but the man was quiet, unobtru-

sive, and did his duties. That was what mattered. "How's it looking up there?"

"Good, real good. We have a clear line of sight all around the perimeter and beyond that, it's just forest. I don't like that part, but the way the owner put concrete all around the house in an oval shape makes this a lot easier to keep an eye on."

"Great," Matteo said as he stirred the pasta. "Dinner's almost ready."

The rest of the night was spent watching television with Marie. Anton went back upstairs to keep watch from there, while Matteo would get up every now and then with the excuse of getting a bag of chips or getting them both drink refills. He wouldn't let her do it, not because he was coddling her, but because he didn't want her to know that he was also keeping a check.

There was no proof that she was in danger, but Anton hadn't been able to trace who the contract came from. To Matteo, that meant it was someone with a lot of power, someone like his aunt. Someone that hadn't yet received what they'd paid for. It was up to him to keep her alive.

The house came with a security system that covered all the windows and doors, as well as a four-foot perimeter outside of the house; they would know if someone tried to get in while they were asleep. That eased some of Matteo's worries and he went to bed with her that night feeling like everything would be okay, for a little while longer.

They cuddled up close together, the air outside was cold, even for the local average from what he'd seen. There'd been a forecast for snow, but they had food for a couple of weeks, plenty of wood, and enough guns in the place to fight off a small army. They'd make do.

He held Marie tightly that night, once she'd fallen asleep, and even when she made to turn over, he followed her with his own body. He needed her heat, her presence, to be able to breathe like a normal human being. She moaned in her sleep, her arm reached for him, and that need for him made his heart swell with pride and with something that he could only describe as adoration.

How had she come to be so important to him? He could admit now that he'd kidded himself when he asked her to marry him, that part where he told them both that he was only doing it to save her. The first time he'd made her come, had that been it?

He could still remember the way she'd clung to him in the pool, soaking wet and completely his. He'd never had anything, or anyone, that had been so completely his. She'd given herself up to him, even if she had no clue who he really was. Maybe because of it.

That was one of the amazing things about Marie, though, her ability to forgive, to adapt, and move on. She wasn't like the other women he knew, always looking for the next big thing, always on the prowl for more. She was happy with what she had, and she let him know it every day with her smile.

Even now, so far from everything they knew, she was adapting already. The palm of his hand slid over the soft flannel of her pajamas to the silky skin beneath it. He wasn't trying to wake her up, all he wanted to do was feel her skin, steal some of her warmth, because even in this cold, she warmed him up. It wasn't desire, though he had plenty of that for her. No, what he felt now was something he remembered feeling a very long time ago, before Celeste, before the word "mafia" was a term he knew. Back when his mother helped him open his Christmas presents and sat his birthday cake in front of him, brightly lit with candles.

The thing Marie brought to him was comfort, and that was something he couldn't let go of. He'd known from the first date with her when they'd only shared coffee at that tiny little café in Louisiana that she could make him smile. She'd brought out something protective in him, that was a given, but she'd also given him a gift he hadn't known he needed. The sensation of being a human that mattered to someone else.

Her eyes had taken him in eagerly, so he'd known there was a sexual attraction there. But the things she asked him, like how he was, if he was doing alright, those were things nobody ever asked him, not even Penelope most of the time. Certainly not Celeste.

For a brief moment, he thought about his mother and her descent into alcoholism. That was Celeste's fault. She'd taken him away from his mother, left her with nothing, and didn't even apologize for it. Not that he knew of anyway. She'd taken away her delightful little boy, the one with the smile that made everyone's heart melt and turned him into a somber, sad little boy that made people look away.

Those that had known him before couldn't stand to look at what Celeste had done to him. The saddest part was not a single one of them had protested, not even his mother. They'd all done what they were told, so long as their accounts were topped up with their monthly allowances. What was one little boy's happiness compared to their desire for wealth and all that came with it?

He'd been abandoned a long time ago, but when Marie came along, he'd finally belonged to someone. That hit him in the gut with a hard punch that nearly made his heart stop. He'd assumed that he'd grow bored with her, but he hadn't, because she showed him what it was to have someone to care for and to be cared for by. He was hers now, not Celeste's, or even his mother's. He belonged to her.

He bent his head to inhale the scent left behind by her shampoo. It was always something that smelled of apples. He loved it, he loved her.

Fuck. He was in trouble in a way he'd never thought possible. Despite his shock at the realization, he stayed close to her. Another sign of just how deeply he was in love with her. He'd never needed to hold anyone before, not like he did Marie. For now, he was comfortable admitting it to himself. Maybe one day he'd tell her, but not now. Not when he needed to stay focused.

Maybe when this was all done, he'd take her somewhere nice, on a warm vacation to the tropics perhaps, and tell her exactly how he felt. Until then, he'd just hold her, keep her safe, and make sure his heart didn't get trampled. As long as he was the only one that knew how much he loved her, his heart was safe, locked inside the cage of his chest where it belonged. One day, when he could, he'd tell her.

## 7

Marie pushed her hand under her pillow and felt her body relax as she absorbed the cool sensation between the sheet and the pillowcase. Why was that so soothing, she wondered but was soon distracted when Matteo slid in beside her. They'd spent the day hauling wood into the house, for the two fireplaces downstairs and the one in their bedroom.

It had been a long job, one that Matteo insisted on doing alone, but she'd put her foot down, literally. She'd stomped her foot she was so mad when he told her he didn't need any help. She smiled at the memory now, at the way he'd laughed before he'd given in and let her come out.

In truth, she'd felt tired and wanted to curl up on the couch and read a book, but it was an opportunity to go outside, so she'd helped him. He'd put his own foot down when she tried to help him carry wood upstairs and had reminded her that she'd had a major surgery not that long ago. She needed to be careful.

She hadn't wanted to admit it, but she was even more tired by then. She'd felt like her arms were about to detach from her body and her feet were frozen solid, she was sure of it, so arguing was pointless. She'd gone into the kitchen, put on a pot of coffee, and waited for him to finish before she made them both a cup and took the mugs into the living room.

It had been a nice day, despite the work, or maybe because of it. She'd had a nap after lunch, and they'd made dinner together.

Those were the only times she saw Anton, at their meals; otherwise, he stayed up there in the attic, keeping watch. He had come down long enough to install cameras on each side of the house before he'd gone back up to watch everything on the television up there. Surely, he must be bored up there? But he didn't complain, he only came down, answered Matteo's questions, ate, then went back upstairs.

Now, she was in bed with her husband and the night was eerily dark. She'd explored the house, although bedrooms and a study weren't that interesting. She'd also found some old books, both fiction and nonfiction, that looked promising. Exhaustion pulled at her, made her yawn as Matteo pulled her close to his warmth. He was like a radiator and she snuggled close to absorb some of his heat.

There was still a chill in the air, even with the fireplace roaring at the other end of the room. A cast-iron screen protected them from sparks or stray pops of over-

heated wood. The sound of the fire crack-
ling at their feet was kind of soothing.

"We never had a proper fire in our
house in Louisiana. There were fireplaces
in the bedrooms upstairs, but we never
used them. I think because Momma had no
idea how to light one."

She was talking now so she wouldn't
think. Throughout the day the tremble in
her pinky finger had come back time and
time again. Her arm had twisted with each
tremble, something new that utterly terrified her. That, along with everything else,
had her in a quiet but panicked mess that
she didn't want to talk about.

Her mother's illness had been masked
for years by her drinking problem. Everything that had gone wrong with her, the
slurred speech, the falls, the tremors, all of
it was put down to alcoholism. Until she fell
that day Marie had tried to escape for the
very first, and only, time. As the daughter
that was left to be the caretaker, Marie had
made it her business to know the signs and

symptoms. She'd made it her business to know what might happen to her mother as time progressed.

She'd learned it was an odd illness that might pop up with one symptom but not another. Some people developed symptoms when they were young, while others would develop it later in life. Much later, like in their 60s later. But here she was, with a tremor, with insomnia, and now, an inability to smell or taste anything.

Matteo hadn't asked her if she was able to smell anything today, and she hadn't volunteered anything. She'd wait until this was over, and she'd go back to see Dr. Murphy. He'd take care of her. There was no need to worry Matteo with this, he had enough on his plate right now.

He hadn't come right out and said it in a while, but they both knew someone had put a contract out on her. Someone wanted her dead. Well, if they waited long enough, the disease would kill her for free, no contract necessary. She'd be the one to pay the price, not whoever wanted her dead.

A tiny little voice, deep down inside, told her it was Celeste. She remembered the way the woman had looked at her the last time they were together. She'd seen the threat in the other woman's eyes, but she didn't want to say anything about that either. She couldn't remember now if she'd told Matteo his aunt had come to visit her. It was before the accident, and some things slipped her mind now. That was one of them.

She rolled into his arms and put her arm over his waist.

"Are you awake?" she whispered softly. She didn't want to wake him up if he was asleep.

"No, my brain just isn't aware of that yet. My body is most definitely asleep." He chuckled as he answered and slid his own arm over to her. He grasped her chin and pulled her face up for a kiss in the shadows cast by the fire. "What's up?"

"Just can't sleep." A groan of frustration accompanied her answer. "I don't want to take any more of those sleeping pills, and I shouldn't need to after today's workout, but I've been here for ages now and my brain won't shut up."

"What's on your mind?" His eyes remained closed, even though he spoke as if he was wide awake too.

"I don't know. A lot of things. I want to go back and have a look at that town where we got groceries if the snow has cleared off the driveway tomorrow. And I'd like to visit some of the sights here. I never thought about coming out here, but I was reading this book today, all about the state and its tourist attractions, and there's quite a bit I'd like to see. How long are we staying?"

"Until the owner tells us to leave, as far as I'm concerned. I'm still connected to New York through email and instant messages, phone calls too, of course. But it's nice out here, not having to drive to ten different places in one day, spending all this time with you. I don't have time for that back home, but out here, I can spend every moment of the day with you."

"It has been nice," she agreed with a grin. "Even if we aren't exactly alone."

"Anton's only watching the perimeter, babe, not us." He rolled over onto his stomach, the way he usually slept, and blew air out softly. "Let's get some sleep."

"Sure, honey," she responded with sympathy. "You get to sleep. You've had a lot of sleepless nights in the last few months."

She wouldn't point out that most of those were over her, or that she hadn't slept well recently either. He didn't need her pointing out the obvious. When his breathing changed and he started to snore softly, she got out of bed and tiptoed downstairs. She wasn't going to sleep, so she might as well read.

She went into the kitchen, poured a cup of juice, took that into the living room, and put the glass down to poke at the fireplace. She added a new log to the embers and waited for the wood to catch before she added another piece. Once the fire was going again, she went to the couch, stretched a blue blanket down over the leather, and then grabbed another thick one made from fleece to put over herself.

She stared at the flames for a moment, lost in thoughts of Matteo. She'd come down to make sure her tossing and turning didn't keep him awake. It was a way of saying I love you, without saying the words, because you didn't always have to say those words to say it. Or so she'd learned in her time with him. He said it when he looked out all of the windows when he thought she wasn't looking, or when he brought her home a dish he wanted her to try from some restaurant she'd never considered going to because she didn't know they existed. He wanted her to try new things and explore the world, and that was his form of I love you.

Even keeping her locked up, or way out here in the middle of nowhere was his version of I love you. She put her head on the pillow with a contented smile and started to read by the light of the fire. She didn't realize she'd fallen asleep until the sound of the alarm woke her up. A loud piercing noise was accompanied by the sound of pounding feet from upstairs. She pushed up off the couch and stood in front of the fire, waiting on one of them to tell her what to do.

"It's alright, it's just a bear," Anton said when he made it down the steps after Matteo.

"A bear?" she asked, her eyes wide. She'd never seen a bear. "Where is it?"

"Yes, Mrs. Mazza, I mean, Marie." He blushed when he said her name, but she ignored it, as she knew he'd appreciate it. "It's a grizzly. I saw it coming on the property but thought it would wander away before it got too close."

The noise suddenly stopped and Matteo came in. "I've turned the alarm off for now. What was it?"

"A grizzly. It might still be out there if you want to see it." Anton went to the living room windows and pointed. "Out there, it pushed against the wooden slats of the fence until a couple broke and it got through. We'll have to go into town tomorrow and get a panel to replace that section."

Marie moved up beside him to look out of the window. The bear had stood up and was scratching its back against another panel of the fence, totally oblivious to the fact that the alarm had gone off, now that it was silent again. Marie held her breath as if even the slightest puff of air against the window would frighten the animal away.

"I didn't know they were that big!" She stared at the furry brown creature in wonder, it was an amazing sight. "They look smaller when they're on all fours, I guess."

"She's a big one," Anton noted as Matteo came up beside Marie to look out at the bear. "Has to be 6 feet tall, at least."

"How much do you think she weighs,"

Marie asked quietly. The animal was huge and looked terrifying, but at the same time, playful as she danced around on the panel, scratching her back good.

"Around 300 pounds," Matteo told her as he looked at the animal.

It was named a grizzly bear, and it was scary to think about an animal so big so close, but Marie didn't feel in danger. Not with the animal outside. Now, in the living room would be another story, but out there, it was just fascinating to watch.

They all laughed when the panel broke under the bear's weight and she flounced off as if insulted. She even cast a look back over her shoulder, as if to shout profanities at it, but she kept going and soon disappeared into the darkness. Marie watched her go with sadness, but she was happy to have seen the large bear.

"Anybody want a drink?" she asked as she headed towards the kitchen at the back end of the house.

"No, I'm going back upstairs. Thanks,

though, Marie." Anton waved at them both before he went back up the pine stairs to restart his vigil.

"Maybe a stiff drink would get me back to sleep. When the alarm went off and you weren't there, I thought I'd have a heart attack." Matteo admitted as he followed her.

"Sorry, I didn't want to disturb you, so I came down here." She poured scotch into two glasses and they took them into the living room. She drank hers down in one gulp and then had a sip of her apple juice to chase the taste away. She still wasn't used to it, but she liked the way it warmed her up.

"Well, it was just a bear, something I hadn't thought about. It was nice to see one though, wasn't it?" Matteo took his time with his drink, savored it as he leaned his head back against the couch.

"It was. I've never seen one. Snakes, nutria, beavers, rats, deer, skunks, alligators, ducks, I've seen all of those. Never a bear, though." She took another drink of her juice and pulled the blanket over her legs.

"What's a nutria?"

"Hmm. Like a mix between a rat and beaver, that's the best way I know how to describe it. Some people make pets out of them. And end up having to buy new furniture if it's wood." She looked at him with a happy tilt to her eyes and took his hand in hers. "Want to go back to bed?"

"Yeah, let's go up. I guess we'll have to go into town now, to replace the panels. Can't have two security breaches, can we?"

"Nope, can't have that at all." Marie grinned up at him as they stood up and headed for the stairs. She let him go up first, just to watch the round swell of his ass as he marched up the steps. Fuck, he had a nice ass. Perfect to hold onto, to cup in your hand and caress, and to just look at when you wanted to see a work of art.

He took an hour out of his morning, almost every day, to work on his body, to keep in shape, and ran for half an hour every evening when he bought her the treadmill. She admired his dedication and the outcome of his efforts. She reached out to pinch his left buttock, then stared up at him innocently when he turned to frown down at her.

"Did you just pinch my ass?" His frown turned to amusement almost immediately.

She blinked up at him, innocence oozing from her pores until she grinned wickedly up at him. She winked at him before she spoke. "Maybe. What are you going to do about it?"

"Oh, Marie," he grinned as he picked her up and carried her into their bedroom. "I'm going to teach you what happens to ladies that pinch men's bottoms. By making you come for an hour."

"Oh, promises, promises," she drawled as a dare, but she knew that was one promise he would most definitely keep.

# 8

They woke up late the next morning, the incident with the bear and the alarm had disturbed their sleep. Matteo watched her as she left the bed in the early morning light. She was a little hunched over as if her back hurt or her stomach. When she came back from the bathroom, he noticed that her hands shook as she brushed her hair.

"Are you alright, Marie?" he asked; concern a gentle tone in his voice.

"Yes, just a little stiff this morning that's all. And tired after that scarc last night." She turned her head just enough to smile at him reassuringly. She turned back to the small mirror over a tall dresser and brushed out her dark hair.

He pushed himself up out of the bed and grimaced when his bare feet touched the floor. "I really need to pick up some slippers or something when we're in town today."

"Oh, we are going out? Good." She flashed him a happy grin and he felt his heart thud in his chest with the pleasure of it. If that's all it took to make her smile like that, theirs would be an easy life. The problem was, she was in danger, so getting smiles like that were more difficult than they should be.

He went out of the bedroom with a slight frown. Maybe they wouldn't have to be so vigilant out here, especially with Anton there to help keep an eye out for threats. Maybe they could relax a little.

His worries were forgotten after he had a shower and went down to breakfast. Marie had biscuits, eggs, and sausage on the table by the time he got down. Anton was seated at the table, quietly eating his food, his eyes on the plate. She was smirking just a little and he knew she was amused with Anton.

Matteo knew the man was a holy terror to any enemies, a loyal employee, and a man to be feared by his other employees. But whenever he was near Marie he turned into a shy man that might be taken for a simpleton. For some reason, that really pleased Marie and he found her amusement amusing. "Good morning, Anton. Sleep yet?"

"Yes, boss." Anton flashed his eyes up at Matteo just long enough for their eyes to meet before they skittered back down to the plate. "I've cleared the car out, and the road looks clear. We can head out after breakfast if you'd like."

"Sounds good to me. How about you, Marie?" Matteo sat down at the table and filled his plate. He saw her eagerly nod her head as he did so and hid a smile.

"That sounds heavenly to me." She

agreed as she picked up her last bite of food. She nodded again as she chewed.

She was so ready to get out into the world that she ran up the stairs to change her clothes, and by the time he finished his food she had on her snow boots and a thick black wool coat. A gray infinity scarf was looped over her head to protect her from the cold and she had on matching gloves. She sat in a chair tapping her foot by the door. Anton was nowhere in sight.

"Eager, aren't we?" He grinned as he teased her, her excitement infecting him.

"I am! Usually, I save that eagerness for you, but I get to be out in the world for a little while, and to see more of the little town we didn't stop long in."

"It's not a big city, a little bigger than your hometown back in Louisiana, but I think there will be plenty to see." He looped a scarf around his neck, put on a wool coat of his own, and slipped on some gloves. "Has Anton gone out to start the car?"

"Yeah, he has." She stood up once he had

a pair of insulated winter boots on and grinned widely. "Ready?"

"Yes, my little bunny." He laughed as she literally began to bounce in place. "Stop or you'll hurt yourself."

"My incision has healed, the doctor cleared me a couple of weeks ago." Matteo had paid dearly for her to have the care of her doctor at their home and he knew she'd been cleared, but he still worried. The incision had been large and she'd had a lot of internal damage from the bullet that had found its mark in her abdomen. "Besides, I need the exercise, come on."

She grabbed her bag, opened the door, and almost skipped out onto the porch. Matteo saw plumes from the exhaust on the black SUV Anton occupied. By the time Matteo took the front seat and Marie had settled into the back, the interior of the car had warmed up. "Everything alright out here?"

"Yep, you ready?"

"We are!" Marie chimed in from the

back and Anton smiled. She couldn't see him but Matteo could. He knew it was respect and shyness that made the big man so timid around Marie, so it was nice to see him smile because of her. That told Matteo that Anton liked her at least.

Anton drove them carefully into the town at the bottom of the mountain and before long they were all busy looking around the many shops and stores.

"Oh, there are quite a few restaurants that look nice here," Marie said and pointed out an Indian restaurant, a few fast-food restaurants, and another that served Chinese cuisine. "There's a lot of shops too, lots more than I expected."

Anton had parked in the parking lot of a strip mall that had a nail salon, a grocery store, a jewelry store, and a small clothing shop. On the other side of the busy street was a large department store that had many more shops attached. There were brightly lit signs all around them and what they'd initially taken to be a small town they could now see was a very large town.

It wasn't a city like New Orleans and definitely not New York, but it was a big town that boasted bars and a theater, as well as quite a few other entertainment places for young and old. Matteo watched Marie look around as Anton headed into the grocery store with a list they'd all prepared. "Do you want to have a look in the shops?"

"Sure, I'd like to go into the grocery store too, but yeah, let's look around?" The smile on her face made her eyes shine and he knew she was genuinely happy to be out in the world. He brushed a lock of dark hair behind her ear and pecked her on the cheek before he took her hand and they walked over to the jewelry store.

There was a necklace in there, some twisted thing of silver and turquoise that caught her eye. It appeared to be two abstract figures of people wrapped around each other with a small bead of turquoise between them. It looked like a globe and the two people had created their own world together. He could see why she was still looking at it.

He was still holding back, still distant when it came to talking of emotional bonds. The way he'd been raised by Celeste had stunted him that way and he couldn't say those three little words to her. He could show her though.

"You know, our anniversary is coming up," he said to her, a hint of a smile on his face with cheeks red from the cold air.

"It is, yes," she whispered then she looked at him. "I can't believe it. We've almost been married for a year now?"

There was surprise on her face, and he could tell she was thinking back over the last year. So many things had happened. So many firsts, new things, scary things, and some that had brought incredible happiness. He saw each moment as a memory came back to her. Her eyes turned from an expression of sadness to happiness, then to wonder, before it settled back to something that might be... contentment? Resignation? He wasn't sure.

"Yes, hard to believe isn't it?" It had been a strange year, and in that time the family business had flourished under his command. Her life, however? Well, she'd been through the wringer since she'd met him. He felt some guilt over that, but at the same time, he knew her life was better.

Even though she'd been attacked, shot even. Even though her mother had passed away, and he'd coerced her into marriage, Marie smiled now. She laughed and she was happy, especially since they'd left New York. Before the attack, she'd done the same thing. She'd started to bloom, to become a young woman that knew her own mind, that had opinions that she'd started to learn to voice. He had improved her life, despite all of the bad things. He knew that.

As he stared down at the pendant on the long silver chain, only about two inches tall, he knew that it was a representation of his life with her so far. Because she'd changed him too. He'd learned what love was in the last year with her. He'd learned that being expressive wasn't a bad thing, even if he still couldn't tell her he loved her. There was a part of him—that little boy afraid of pain, of being punished for showing emotion by having food denied to him, by being sent to sleep in the coldest room in the house for seeking to see his mother so that he could have some kind of motherly love—that held him back from taking that next step.

But that pendant would show her. They'd become one over the space of time that they'd been a married couple, they'd overcome and forged a bond that he was certain nothing could break. Celeste would come back eventually, and if she hadn't put this contract out on his wife, then she might want to hand over the reins entirely to him. If not, he'd walk away with his own businesses well in hand and live his life with the woman that made him… happy.

"Let's get it." The price-tag was not

cheap, but he didn't care. He had plenty of cash on him and they could afford it.

"Really?" She breathed out the words like she couldn't believe him, the first glimmer of excitement in her eyes.

"Really, come on." He tugged at her hand and before she knew it, the cold silver of the chain slid down her collar bones and into the space just above her cleavage. She held it in her palm, looked into the mirror the jeweler had placed on the counter, and grinned with genuine pleasure. "It's beautiful, Matteo, thank you."

"Well, I wanted to get you something monumental for our anniversary anyway and this is just perfect really, isn't it?" He kissed the back of her neck where he'd pushed her hair away to fasten the necklace and then stepped around to look at her. "Happy?"

"More than I could have ever dreamed of." She leaned up, kissed him quickly, and turned back to the mirror. "It's perfect."

"Wear it always as a symbol of my

promise to you, Marie. I will always be with you, I will do all that is in my power to protect you, and I will always, always work to make you my world. Always, baby." He felt something swell in his chest as he spoke to her, some emotion that made it hard to breathe, to finish the rest of what he wanted to say.

"I will, Matteo. I will." She put her arms around him and the tension eased. He could breathe again, and the world slowly came back into focus. The jewelry store owner made a sound and they turned to look at the woman.

"I knew when I made that piece that it would find the right home." The woman with light-red hair and warm brown eyes turned to them. "I can tell you two are special. I didn't know it, but I made that piece just for you. I can see it."

"You mean this is the only one?" Marie asked with a sound of stunned awe in her voice after what the woman had said.

"Yes, I make one of a kind pieces for the

store. I don't know who exactly it's for when I make it, but I know every piece of jewelry I make will find the right home." Her eyes had taken on a far-away look as if there was something mystical calling to her. Her long silk skirt and the matching sapphire-blue silk scarf tied around her hair, gave her a witchy, but appealing, air.

"Thank you, I believe you're right. It's perfect for us both." Matteo reached out his hand to shake the woman's fragile, almost bird-like hand before he turned back to his wife. "Right, well, now let's go find Anton and get some groceries."

"That sounds like a good idea." Marie agreed and gave the jewelry maker a broad grin. "Thank you for making this for me."

"It was my pleasure," the woman said softly as they left the store hand in hand.

Matteo looked around as they left the shop behind and walked down to the grocery store. He was always vigilant when he left the safety of a confined space but even more so when Marie was with him. He didn't learn to be that way after the attack, it had come naturally once she became his wife, but now he felt even more determined to keep an eye out for any danger. She deserved every ounce of devotion and vigilance he gave her.

# 9

"There are turkeys outside," Marie said to Matteo the next morning as he walked into the kitchen. "Four females and a male."

"How do you know the difference?" he asked with mirth in his voice, as if he was always amazed and amused by the things she knew.

"Females, the hens, have lighter colored skin on their heads. The males will have red and blue looking skin. And then there's obviously the feathers when they puff up to attract the females. This one had a moment where he walked around, dragging his feathers in the snow."

"I see," he muttered as he walked over to the window to look out at the small group of turkeys still out there, scratching around in the snow. "Should we put some sort of food out for them?"

"I don't think so. They might get used to it and that wouldn't be good." She looked down at the sausage she had frying in a pan and tried not to think about how long they'd be there before they went back to New York.

Even with Anton in the attic above them all day, it still felt peaceful, quiet, like it was just them two. He'd disappear into the room he'd made an office for a while off and on throughout the day, but he was still there, and she loved that. They'd never spent so much time together and while it was hard to hide the things she didn't want him to see with him always there, she'd managed so far.

One of those things was how the tremor

in her pinky finger had spread to her whole right hand. It even traveled up her arm sometimes, but so far, she'd been able to keep it from him. She'd put her arm behind her back, or under her head, or turn that part of her body away from him when she felt it. But that didn't mean it wasn't there, that the worry wasn't there.

"Have you never hunted before?" she asked as she checked on the biscuits in the oven, mainly as a way to distract herself from her own thoughts. He answered as she pulled the golden-brown buttermilk biscuits from the oven.

"No, it's not something my family ever really participated in, as far as I know. We're city people and our food has always come from a butcher or a grocery store. We don't kill wild animals for sport either." Something in his tone told her that there was more to that last sentence, something along the lines of: "we don't kill wild animals that are human unless they cross us in some way".

She didn't want to think about that either, right now, and turned to the sausage now finished in the pan. "Do you want gravy with breakfast, or shall we just have sausage biscuits with scrambled eggs?"

"Sausage biscuits are fine." He poured three glasses of orange juice and set them on the table as Anton came into the kitchen.

"It smells lovely, as always," the big man said as he went to sit in his usual chair, at the other end of the rectangular table.

The room was filled with windows so there was plenty of natural light as the sun streamed down onto snow that reflected it back with bright, piercing beams. It was too cold for the snow to melt but the sun tried to do its job.

Marie set the food down onto the table and sat quietly as the men discussed security. They'd repaired the fence the bear had broken in through the day before and had checked the rest of the perimeter. The only way anyone could slip in now was through the gate, which was basically just a cattle gate, meant to keep vehicles out. That's how the turkeys had gotten in, Marie thought as she glanced out of the window in front of the table.

"I called the owner and he said we can replace the gate if we want to, at our expense of course," Anton told Matteo as he placed scrambled egg onto the biscuit and then a piece of sausage. He glanced up at Matteo and then, swiftly, at Marie.

She hid a smile behind her biscuit as she took a bite. He was getting used to being around her. That was good. She had started to feel bad for him, that he had to be around her so much when it obviously made him uncomfortable. He was coming around, though, and that was a good thing.

"You going to run into town and get that?" Matteo asked as he built another biscuit, then went to the fridge to bring back slices of cheddar.

Marie took one of the slices and assembled her own biscuit. "If you're going into town, can you stop at the store and get a beef roast? I think I'd like to cook one for dinner."

She'd found a slow cooker in one of the cabinets earlier and wanted to use it. Matteo had already banned her from wood-carrying duty for the day because it was so cold, so she needed something to fill her time. She could only do so much knitting and reading could consume days, but none of the books she'd bought really grabbed her now that she was back at the cabin. Maybe a day of cooking would do her some good.

"Sure, Marie." Anton nodded and smiled at her quickly, before he looked away, his face now red because their eyes had come together. That poor man, she thought and got up from the table.

"I'll get everything started here for dinner and put the meat in when you get back then."

She put the dishes in the dishwasher and cleaned up the kitchen while the men got ready to get on their way.

Matteo would spend a couple of hours bringing in firewood while Anton was gone. Marie watched him for a moment from one of the windows, long after Anton had gone, and wondered at how strong he was. He might be a city boy, but he worked hard, all day long.

She admired the way his body moved as he brought in armfuls of wood, even under the thick coat he'd found in town. It was a black, insulated coat, typical of those in the farming community because it was able to keep the wearer warm, even in the coldest of temperatures. It wasn't the kind of coat he'd wear at any other time in his life, she knew, but it suited him, she thought. The black knit cap on his head did things to her too, to her insides that were always on alert around him.

The black cap made his eyes stand out to her in ways that just made her feel... squishy. Like her insides had turned to mush and if she looked at him too long, she'd forget words. All of them. She turned away from the window now and went to prepare the vegetables she'd use in the pot roast. She'd found a recipe she wanted to try and wanted to make sure she had everything before Anton came back. She'd call him from the house phone if she needed something.

She reached to take carrots out of the crisper drawer in the fridge and moaned as her entire arm started to shake. The moan was from fright, anger, and frustration - all three mixed into panic. She'd have to tell him soon, mainly because she needed to go to the doctor. Maybe it was nerve damage, something from the attack, or some psychological problem. It might not be the one thing she dreaded the most - her mother's illness.

As she glanced back at the window to make sure Matteo couldn't see her, she felt the tremor become stronger, until she couldn't even control the limb. Fuck.

"Fuck," she screamed quietly. "Please, stop. Just… stop."

Fear gripped her throat then, filled it with a lump that she couldn't breathe past, then the world started to go fuzzy and she saw sparkles. She knew it was panic, that she was about to faint, so she moved back to the island to slide down to the floor. "Breathe, just breathe."

That's what the counselor told her during one of their sessions. Whenever you have a problem, whenever you feel over-whelmed, he'd said, "Just breathe, Marie. That's all you have to do is breathe." She clutched at the necklace that rested on her chest and focused on it. Matteo had said it was his promise to her, to always protect her. But he couldn't protect her from the disease she was almost certain she was de-veloping, nobody could.

Would he want her if she turned out like her mother? She doubted she'd ever be as bitter and twisted as her mother, but her body would twist, it would become something she couldn't control. Would he want a wife like that? Would it be fair to burden him with that? He had enough troubles.

She took one more deep breath and looked down at her hand. The tremor had slowed down, calmed enough that she could flex her fingers. *You can do this, Marie.* That was the mantra she repeated in her mind. With a wince, she got up and went back to the fridge. *Just breathe.*

She pulled out the vegetables she'd need, found the herbs and spices, and started to cut up the vegetables. She went slowly, to make sure the very sharp knife was away from her fingers when she made each cut. She closed her eyes each time she made a cut and opened them once the blade hit the cutting board. Each new cut brought a sigh of relief.

The need to distract her mind became overwhelming, so she went to a small radio on the counter and turned it on. Rock music filled the air, some station that only played 80s rock, so she sang along with Stevie Nicks and Bob Segar as she prepared the onions and started to caramelize them.

Matteo came in to have a cup of coffee about the time she took the onions off and put them in a bowl to use later. "Hi, babe. How ya doing?"

"I'm fine, honey." She pecked his cheek as he passed her and then put the rest of the vegetables in containers to put in the fridge. She'd peeled potatoes and sliced them, along with celery and carrots. Now all she needed was the meat. She'd sear it with some red wine and put that all together in the slow cooker when Anton came back.

With a sigh of relief, she poured a cup of coffee for herself and went to sit with Matteo at the table. "Want some lunch?"

"I'll just have a sandwich in a little while." He glanced at the clock and frowned. "Anton will be home soon."

"Yeah. Why is that a bad thing?"

"Because I was watching you as you put all of that away, and I don't know, all I could think about was pressing you up against the fridge and kissing you until you couldn't stand up straight."

"Oh?" Her eyebrows went up with amusement. "I was watching you earlier. I wondered if it was too cold to jump you in the snow. But there's snow, of course it's too cold."

"Hmm. Maybe we should meet up after lunch, maybe in our bedroom. If we turn the television on he won't hear a thing."

"You might be right." He could always make her smile and now was no exception. It was just that the smile was dirty, in that naughty kind of way, she could feel it, but couldn't wipe it off of her face.

Her fingers reached out for his, and she leaned across the space between their chairs to meet his lips with hers. His silky tongue came out to tease her bottom lip, to ask her to open for far more. With a growl, he moved, lifted her from the chair to put her on the table. "Or I could just fuck you right here."

"You could." She was already pushing

her pink pajama pants down. "You so could, Matteo."

"Open," he demanded as he bent to kiss her again.

With a kick of her feet, she pushed the pants away and opened her mouth at the same time. She was more than ready for him when he slid into her, both her mouth and the part of her that yearned for him the most. She gave a sigh of relief as she felt his entire length sink into her.

The groan he couldn't hold back sent a shiver down her spine, but they didn't have a lot of time. Anton would be back soon. They didn't want to be caught. "Hurry, baby. Please, hurry."

He slid his lips from hers, down her neck, to that spot just behind and beneath her ear that made her go boneless. The warm skin of his hand slid between them as he sought out the small spot that would send her into space. With a firm pressure, he circled her clit, until her head pushed at his, her lips open for his kiss.

"Tell me," he demanded as he looked down at her. His hips slid into her at a slow pace, slow and steady as his finger worked at her with an unrelenting pace. "Say it, Marie."

"Kiss me, Matteo." She uttered the words smoothly, but she wasn't sure she sounded in control. She had little self-control where he was concerned.

The sound of tires on snow made him tense up and he looked down at her. "Don't stop. Come for me, Marie."

"But..." he didn't let her finish. He kissed her again, he circled faster, drove himself deeper into her walls, until she grunted as bliss shot through her lower organs and up into her brain. He came with her, quickly, but with a satisfied grunt. It was only moments before he'd straightened up, rearranged his clothes, and went to the kitchen door.

"Get your breath back. I'll bring in the groceries after I help him unload that gate."

A subtle wink made her grin just before she collapsed on the table in shock.

It had happened so quickly, but it was oh so satisfying. She jerked up when she heard the front door open and giggled like a schoolgirl as she slid her pants back on. Nervous fingers smoothed her hair back into a neat bun while she walked back to the stove. With a deep breath that came out on a sigh, she found a pot to sear the beef in before she put it in the slow cooker.

She couldn't stop the smile on her face, but she did notice a tremor in her legs as she walked around the kitchen. That was all Matteo though, it didn't have anything to do with her problems. Not a thing at all.

# 10

---

"Matteo, how long are we going to stay out here? Not that I'm complaining, but I'd like to make a couple of appointments and I don't know anyone out here." She spoke to him in bed later that evening, some gameshow from England played on You-Tube on the television, but she couldn't concentrate on it.

Her arm had gone all spastic again when she showered earlier. She'd had to stay in the shower until the hot water had almost run out before it stopped. Now, she was trying to find a way to ask him without giving anything away.

"What appointments, darling?" he asked absently as he watched the contestant on the screen make a stupid choice and scoffed at them. "Idiot."

"Just things like my hair and stuff." She didn't want to say she wanted to go back to New York to see the doctor. She didn't want him to worry, not unless there was a reason for it. For now, it would be best to keep her worries to herself.

"You can get your hair done in town." Absently, still, he reached for her hair. "It looks fine anyway. What do you want to be done to it?"

"Just a trim." Her eyes went back to the screen, but she couldn't stop the way she pulled her lip in between her teeth. Or the way she frowned. He hadn't actually answered her.

Sometimes she still felt like a prisoner because he wouldn't answer questions she had. He'd deflect, change the subject, or make some other comment that just wasn't an answer. It was like she was on house arrest, with only the illusion of freedom.

She frowned at her thoughts, which weren't really fair. He was trying to keep her safe, and not just because she'd been attacked. The aftermath had been rough on her, the gunshot, the ensuing internal damage, the surgery, the healing, it had all been rough on someone that had been through so much already. The stress had been immense and, luckily, he was quite aware of that.

He knew she wasn't used to such cold temperatures either. Even if she'd spent the last winter in New York, it felt different out here, like something that you couldn't escape sometimes. The bathroom had been cold earlier, so cold she hadn't wanted to get into the shower. Then she didn't want to get out of it, even though her hand had stopped trembling. The cooling of the water forced her out, though.

That meant she was a prisoner of the

cold, a prisoner of Matteo's worries, and a prisoner of her recent worries, too. The urge to get up and pace hit her, but she didn't want to get out of the warmth of the down duvet on the bed. Matteo had found it in the closet and put it on the bed this afternoon. It made getting into the bed heavenly after her shower.

Instead of getting up to walk around the house, she turned to her husband. "Matteo?"

"Yes?" He was still watching the show and didn't turn to look at her. Hmmm.

A quick wiggle of her right hand told her that her fingers were warm, so she slid them across his stomach until she reached the top of his pajama pants. The black fleece easily pulled away from his skin and he looked down at her, his attention now solely focused on her and where her pinky was. "Hi there."

"Oh, you see me now?" She grinned up at him from his right side, her chin on his chest.

"I do indeed. How could I miss you when you're being so... exploratory?" His words came out quietly, even though they were well away from the space Anton inhabited in the attic above. Matteo was a private man in many ways. Even if he liked to press his luck by continuing to fuck her just as Anton came back, as he'd done earlier.

"How long," she paused to slide her hand lower, "are we staying in Montana?"

His breath caught and his eyebrows rose as she found his very hard cock. He was always ready for her, at even the slightest touch. Even just a few words could bring his body to life, which was something she dearly loved about him.

"Oh, I don't know. Until the threat is neutralized, or before that maybe. It just depends on how quickly we find out who put the contract out." The last of his sentence came out as a gasp as she began to stroke him with her hand.

"Right. So, I could make a few appointments here?" She waited for him to nod his head before she pulled away. "Thanks. That's all I needed to know."

The evil but naughty grin on her face as she pulled her hand out of his pants made him turn suddenly and pull her beneath him. "Is that how it is? You try to seduce me to get the information you want and once you have it, you just leave me to suffer?"

"Oh no, darling," Marie replied as she put her arms around his neck. "I knew exactly what would happen, and this is it."

She didn't get to say anything else because his mouth covered hers as the passion grew into flames between them. She'd think about it all tomorrow. For now, all she could think about was him.

THE NEXT FEW days were taken up with installing the new security gate, bringing in more wood, and watching films on Netflix. She watched an entire series in one sitting some days. Sometimes, if it wasn't too cold out, Matteo would walk around the property with her, just for the exercise.

They used a virtual private network to hide their location when they were online, a really good one that cost a pretty penny or a dozen, so she was able to talk to Trina sometimes, even if she wasn't allowed to tell her where they were. It was nice to hear another voice, but still, the worries over her condition she kept to herself. Trina might tell Matteo, and she wasn't ready to bring that subject up again.

She'd bought a kit at the store the last time she was in town, a kit that promised she would have one perfectly crocheted hat when she was finished, and she worked on that while she watched television. It wasn't the perfect example shown in the picture, and she'd had to watch some videos online to find out exactly what one of the stitches was, but she got through it.

When she'd seen the kit, she thought it might improve her fine motor skills, and keep her arms moving. The whole thing was an attempt to stave off what she saw as a threat to her whole life. If she could just keep her balance, her range of motion, she could beat the disease. Marie knew it didn't work like that, but there wasn't much else she knew to do.

Matteo often asked her what was troubling her, he knew something was, but she didn't want to talk about it. They were playing rummy, watching the snow fall outside of the kitchen windows when he brought it up again.

"What's troubling you, Marie? You keep brushing me off, but you sigh a lot for a woman that's got nothing on her mind." He placed a card on the pile that she needed to make a trio of threes, so she took it and put the trio down, which left her with one card.

"I want to see a doctor. I think maybe I have a pinched nerve in my neck, something like that." She finally admitted something, though it wasn't exactly what her problem was. Well, not what her fears were.

"Does it hurt?" he asked, his brows

knitted together as he leaned towards her? "Maybe some ice, or heat, would help?"

"No, it doesn't hurt. My arm just keeps going... numb." She looked down at her remaining card, afraid he'd see the truth in her eyes.

"Oh, okay. Well, I'm sure there's a doctor in town that can have a look at you." He pulled a card from the pile and looked at what was in his hand. "It sounds like a trapped nerve to me, if it's going numb."

"Yeah," she answered and felt stupid because that was all she could think to say. She sighed again and stared out of the window while he decided what to do with his cards. Her free hand came up to touch the necklace he'd given her. It was so special to her and touching it brought her a lot of comfort.

"You're a really sweet man for such a tough guy, Matteo." She changed the subject entirely and looked back at him as he put down a four that she didn't need. She reached for another card and threw it away.

"What do you mean?" he murmured absently as he stared at the long line of cards and then looked at the one card that remained in her hand. She could tell he was wondering if he should take the cards he needed and hope she didn't throw her last card and go out, or whether he should leave the cards and hope for something better. It was all chance, much like their lives now. And even in a game of chance, he weighed every option, keenly aware that she was on the brink of winning. It was the same way he approached life. Was the choice he had to make worth the risk?

His eyes came up to her, comically narrowed into slits of suspicion before he made his move. He took three cards from the pile and laid down a trio, which left him with four more in his hand. She smiled at him, gave him a wink, picked up a card, and weighed her own options.

Place the card that matched her trio of twos down with the others, or let him have a chance to catch up to her score? Hmm.

She looked up at him, saw the uncertainty there, and decided to let him have one more chance at it. She threw the card she'd been holding in her hand down on the discard pile, and waited to see if he'd pick it up. She'd noticed he'd collected two jacks, so he must need the one she'd held.

With a grin of triumph, Matteo picked up the card and threw another one on the discard pile, which left him with one card in his hand. They were evenly matched now, so when she took the next card and it played on his jacks, she put it down with the rest of her, along with her card that matched the twos, and grinned at him.

"Floating," she whispered with wide eyes, a mock evil expression of triumph on her face.

"That's not a thing, you either go out, or you don't," he said immediately, but he didn't look certain.

"That's not how I learned to play it. This is how Trina taught me to play," she countered and dared him to question it with a playful glare.

"Hmph. She cheats anyway. Well, I guess since we're playing by your rules, you're floating. Does that mean I pick another card up?" His dark eyebrows were up now in question.

"It does." She nodded. She'd been bored with the game, almost too consumed by her own worries to enjoy the moment, but the last few plays had brought her around. She would have enough points to beat him now, and it was very rare to beat Matteo at any kind of game.

"Fine." He pretended to be offended and picked up a card with a very snooty expression. "There, I can't go out."

He put the card he'd picked up down on the discard pile and she picked up one of her own from the pickup pile. It matched her trio of kings, so she put it down on that pile and put down the last card in her hand. "Done."

"It's only because you cheated." He

mock-pouted and collected the cards to shuffle them up. "Trina has taught you some very bad rules, I have to say."

"No, I think you're just a sore loser!" She got up from the table to get a glass of apple juice and asked if he wanted anything.

"A bottle of water, please. Is there any more of that salsa you made, the one with cheese? That was nice."

"There is, it'll take a minute to reheat it." She pulled out everything she needed, felt a tremor go through her arm as she pulled plastic from the bowl of salsa, and paused to wait it out.

"What's wrong?" He'd noticed the way she'd stopped, but then, he was very ob-servant.

"Nothing, just my arm going numb again." She dismissed it all, but he got up to come over to her.

"Let me do it then. I forgot about that. Let me help, Marie." He gently nudged her out of the way, and she was grateful he did. He might notice that her arm was shaking if he hadn't. It wasn't numb at all, not really, it was a tremor that she couldn't control.

"Thanks. I'll get a couple of bowls and a bag of nachos."

The snow outside was only piling up, but Anton had gone into town to get more food the day before. There was plenty of firewood and the power was on. There was a generator at the back of the house, in case the power went off, so everything was great. She was just stuck inside again.

At least this time she could go outside if she wanted to. It was the weather that trapped her today, not her husband. She watched as Matteo put the salsa in the microwave, and how careful he was when he brought it back to the table. He was just as careful with her.

"Why are you always so... *precise*?" she stressed the word, paused, and nodded. "Yes, 'precise' is the right word. Why is that?"

"Celeste wasn't an easy woman to be around," he started. Every now and then he'd slip something about his childhood into the conversation, or he'd answer a question she had. Most of the time he'd change the subject quickly, but she understood that. "I learned to be very careful - to not spill, break, or drop anything around her."

"She sounds like my mother. It was alright for her to throw things, break things, but if I got one thing wrong, I had hell to pay."

"You understand then." He slipped into the chair opposite her where they sat in the middle of the table. He put the glass bowl down on a potholder with a large spoon in it. "We had very similar childhoods, in many ways, I think. Only, your mother was ill; my aunt was just a scary bitch that liked to torture me in the name of making me a man. The kind of man she wanted me to be."

"Lucky for me you still have a mind of your own." She dipped some of the salsa into her bowl and pulled out a nacho chip.

"As do you." He smiled as he relaxed and ate their snack. "It's amazing we aren't completely broken, you now?"

"We adapted, both of us, in our own ways, I guess," Marie volunteered, her eyes far away, her memories somewhere in the past. "My mother used to hate it that I could just turn off and put up with her. Sometimes, when I was little, thought she wanted to make me run away from home. But if I tried to leave, she'd always drag me back one way or another."

"Like when you tried to go to LSU?" he asked, his eyes watchful, curious.

"Yeah, but even when I was younger. She used to tell me that if I called child protective services on her, or told the teachers about how she used to hit me and stuff, that she'd hunt me down and bring me back, no matter what." Marie shivered as memories flooded in, painful ones. "I couldn't understand it. She hated me, told me every day, in very plain language, that she hated my every existence. Yet, she didn't want to let me go."

"I guess she wanted to have you as her whipping boy, so to speak. Without you, who else would she have to abuse, to complain to, to blame?" Matteo felt the way her eyes cut to him, sympathy in her gaze.

"It was the same for you, I guess?"

"In a way, yes. Celeste didn't tell me she hated me, or that I should have been aborted, but she was cruel. At least, until I learned what exactly she wanted me to be, to act how she wanted me to act. I remember once, she'd rewarded me with a puppy, a tiny little thing that followed me around all the time. When it was six months old, it had an accident in the house because I was in bed ill and hadn't been able to let him out. She had him euthanized."

"Fuck, Matteo." The wrenching pain his words caused her was apparent in her voice as she spoke. "That's awful."

She found his hand with hers and held on, even after he smiled and pushed the

memory away. "She taught me responsibility."

"What an awful way to do it." She
frowned. "Isn't she due back soon?"

"I think so. But her last email said she
might stay a few more months, so I don't
know. Apparently, Italy suits her."

"We can hope." Marie went back to
munching on salsa and chips. "If we're
lucky, she'll not come back at all."

The words just slipped out, and she felt
terrible for it, but he just laughed it off. "I
have to agree with you. She's a terrible
person."

"She is, yeah." The need to hide her embarrassment at her brash words made her
look away. "It's stopped snowing."

"Want to build a snowman?" he asked
with a twinkle in his eye.

"Isn't that from a movie or something?"

"It is, but I've never seen it. I've just seen
it on so much merchandise."

"I think I would like to build a snowman

with you." She finished her salsa and got up. "I'll get dressed."

"I'll meet you outside then."

She had on plaid flannel pajamas, so she went up to change into leggings, a pair of jeans, and a thick gray sweatshirt that she pulled on over a long-sleeved t-shirt. That ought to keep her warm. Downstairs, she put on her coat, gloves, her new crocheted cap in awful shades of pink and green, and a scarf.

They worked together to build three giant balls of snow, then he went off to find some branches to make the limbs with while she sought out small rocks for his face. "We don't have a top hat to put on him."

"No, but I don't think he needs one." Matteo stood back to examine the newly decorated, if somewhat plain, snowman. "Not a bad job for your first snowman."

"How did you know that?" She looked at him quizzically.

"You grew up in Louisiana, there wasn't

anywhere to build one in New York, and you haven't built one since we've been here. Logic tells me you have never made one."

"You're right." She laughed and flopped back onto the ground. "I've never made snow angels either."

He laughed at her comical movements as she thrashed her arms up and down at her sides. "How do you know how to make one then?"

"I've seen it in movies and stuff." She very carefully stood up and walked away from the spot. "Not bad."

"Not bad at all." He got up and looked down at the pair of snow angels. A wary look came over his face when he turned to her. He had his hand behind his back. "I guess you've never had a snowball fight either?"

"Don't you dare," Marie cried as he lobbed a handful of snow at her face. "You dick!"

She screeched as some of the snow made its way down her scarf and onto her neck. She grabbed up a handful of snow, ran behind the snowman, and patted the snow into a ball. He'd had time to form a few more and lobbed them at her as she came out long enough to throw one snowball.

She laughed loudly when it hit him right in the chest and exploded.

"Oh, I'll get you for that!" he called out and ran behind the car parked out front.

She ignored him as she made snowballs quickly and stuffed two each into her pockets. She had one in her hand when she broke cover and ran for the other end of the SUV. He must not have seen her move because he came around the hood to throw snowballs at the snowman. She got him with one right in the side of his head, and it broke apart on his black knit cap.

"Fuck!" he cried out when the snowball fell apart and he realized she'd got him from somewhere different. "Sneaky little cow!"

She laughed a delighted sound and ran

for the other side of the car as he chased her. He was still chasing, so she threw a snowball back at him but he ducked that one. The next one caught him, but he also caught her. "Gotcha."

"No fair! I still have snowballs left." She tripped over something under the snow and fell to the ground. They were rolling around in the snow, giggling and kissing when Anton came outside.

"You two alright?" he asked as he looked down at them doubtfully from the porch.

"What? Yeah, we just came out to play in the snow," Marie said right before she lobbed a snowball in his direction. It struck him right on the left shoulder and he looked down as if stunned.

His green eyes met her brown ones in complete shock. "Well, I guess this means war."

The words came out as if he'd just pronounced war on a country, so serious, but with a tiny glint of humor that made his lips twitch.

"Oh shit," Matteo whispered. "Get up, come on, get up."

They both laughed as they ran for the other side of the cabin and started to build snowballs together. It was like being a kid she thought, playing in a way she'd never been able to play when she was a child. It was incredibly... fun.

"Are you ready for the pain?" Anton called out and Marie scooted to the edge of the cabin to look out. He'd built some kind of wall along the top of the hood of the SUV out of the snow and she could see him standing there. "Oh shit, Matteo. He's built a fort!"

"No shit?!" he asked and joined her. "Well, I'll be damned, he has. That sneaky cu... uh, bastard."

"What do we do?" She turned to ask him just as Anton made his first shot, one that clocked her right in the back of the hood. "Fuck you, Anton! You're little fort is going down!"

"Try it, sister. You can't defeat me." The

little boy in him had come out to play, obviously, and she could swear she even heard him snort with laughter.

"Here, take these, aim for his fort." Matteo had quickly made up some rather hard-packed snowballs and Marie started to throw them, one after another. Several hits, but they just joined to the wall without damaging it.

"I don't think that's going to work," she turned to tell him. Another snowball smacked her in the back of the head softly when she did.

"Score two for me, none for you!" Anton called out with glee.

"That fucker," Marie hissed with mock anger. "What do we do now?"

"Follow me." Matteo took her hand and they ran around the edge of the house to the other side. "Get behind me."

"Why?" she asked, a little miffed that he wanted to go first.

"Because he's going to hit me first, so if you're behind me, you can get him next."

Matteo grinned down at her. "Then we'll both get him."

"Good planning!" She grinned and followed him as he ran for the edge of the SUV.

They spent another ten minutes throwing snowballs back and forth, and they were all covered in snow by the time Marie fell to the ground, exhausted from laughing and the cold. The sun had started to go down and the temperature had dropped even more.

"I think it's time we get her inside, boss," Anton said as the two men looked down at her. They were grinning just as much as she was.

For a moment, it felt like the world narrowed down to just this moment in time, this moment of pure happiness and fun, and she knew it was a memory she'd never forget. Matteo held out his hand and pulled her up off the ground. "Yeah, I think it's time for cocoa and something a little alcoholic to warm us up. Come on, my little snow bunny, let's get you warm."

Her nose, chin, and cheeks were glowing from exertion and the cold air, but she didn't care. She was happy, and so were the men. They tramped into the cabin, pulled off their winter gear, and she ran up to put her pajamas back on but left her hat on. She'd kind of grown to like the silly thing and it helped her to feel warm.

She walked back downstairs to find the men had boiled water in the kettle and put out three mugs of hot cocoa with a plate of buttered toast for all of them. She smiled at them both because she felt they'd broken down some barrier with Anton. He smiled back and nodded at her cup.

"That one is yours." He spoke directly to her for the first time, almost like a brother, and that made something warm begin to glow in her chest.

"Thanks, Anton." She leaned into Matteo for a moment, as a way to say hello to him, and then picked up a slice of toast. "That was fun."

"It was," Matteo agreed quickly and sat back in his chair. "I don't think I've played like that since I was very small."

"We did it all the time where I grew up in upstate New York," Anton volunteered, which shocked them both. Neither spoke, and Marie knew Matteo kept quiet for the same reason she did: any words might stop him. "Up until high school, anyway. Then we all became too cool for children's games. I don't know why we thought that it's fun."

He didn't look at either of them, just his cup of cocoa, but he smiled as he continued. "We'd get some major snowstorms up there. Sometimes the snow would be so high we couldn't open one of the doors. Those days were pretty boring, but we got by."

Marie nodded before she spoke, "For us, it was flooding that would trap us. Luckily, Mom's house was built on higher ground, but the water would come up around the sides sometimes, up to the steps, and all the animals outside would try to swim in. Which can be dangerous when it's snakes, spiders, and animals scared out of their minds."

"I bet that was scary," Anton agreed. "I've seen it on television, the way it floods down there. I think I'd want to build my house on a hill."

"There aren't many hills in southern Louisiana," Marie laughed. "You can build the ground up, but you have to let it settle for a really long time before you build on it or put another layer on."

"I've heard some people reclaim land from the swamp. Wouldn't that just get all soggy again eventually?"

"Not if you do it right." Marie frowned but carried on. "I don't know a lot about how they do that, but the engineers have found ways of doing it."

"What are we planning for dinner?" Matteo interrupted the silence that followed.

"Chili?" Marie offered, but Anton broke in.

"I'd like to make dinner tonight if it's alright with you two?" He looked at them and smiled when they nodded. "Cool. I'm going to make a goulash, so I'd best start it now. It'll take a while, you reckon everything will be okay while I'm down here, Matteo?"

"Should be. We'll both be keeping our eyes peeled." Matteo stood up and stretched. Marie caught a glimpse of his abdomen as his flannel shirt rode up, and wished she could touch him there, but Anton might run back up to his attic haven if she did. She clenched her fingers and looked at Matteo. "I'll see if I can get an appointment with a doctor, there should be one in town."

"If they're open," he reminded her. "There's a phone book in the living room, have a look in there."

"I will," she promised, even though she'd already done that. She'd picked up the phonc to call the one she'd found a dozen times, but never dialed the number. Fear had always made her put the number away. She owed it to him to find something out, though, and to herself.

She'd have to stop putting it off and face facts, she decided. She could stay in this prison forever, and let it grow worse, or find out if she even had the disease at all. If she did, maybe there was a cure for it that had been newly discovered or at least something that could stave off the worse symptoms. She followed him out of the kitchen, but when he split off to go to the office, she went into the living room, her eyes on the table by the couch where she'd hidden the number in a drawer. She could do this.

## 11

Matteo stared at his computer screen, fear a tight knot in his stomach. Nerve damage, stress, maybe she'd damaged her shoulder when she was attacked. They were all thoughts that flitted through his mind as he stared blankly into space. With a sigh of frustration, he got up and walked over to the window in the small office.

He picked up a pair of binoculars that rested on a small table next to the window and looked out towards the edge of the fence. He'd noticed she spent a lot of time staring out of the windows as if lost in her own thoughts, or searching for answers that she never found. She didn't know it, but he spent a lot of time staring out of the windows too. Only he wasn't looking for answers, he was looking for threats.

He thought about the last email he'd received from Celeste, a few days ago. There'd been an odd shortness in her email. Normally she'd go on about how wonderful life was in Italy, how people were much more refined than back home, but this time, she'd written three simple lines.

*Not sure when I'm coming home.*

*I may be a few more months.*

*I heard you'd disappeared, where are you?*

He hadn't responded yet. He didn't know how to respond, because as every day passed, as memories bombarded his dreams and his waking moments, he became more convinced that it was Celeste that had ordered that contract. Anton had people working on it but as of yet, the author of that contract had not been identified. Normally, it wouldn't take long, which was something else that told him this was Celeste. The woman knew how to cover her tracks, or she wouldn't still be the head of the family.

It didn't take a lot of skills to know that Marie was worried. She'd spoken about her worries before, but earlier this morning she'd tried to deflect from those worries, to blame the reason for her tremors on something else. He couldn't blame her for that and knew she did it only to keep him from worrying, but she should know by now that he was always worried for her. There was a real possibility that she could have Parkinson's disease.

That disease would ruin her life in many ways, it would even take her life eventually. The fact that she was so young and already showing signs was exceedingly worrisome. He'd done research many, many times. He'd looked for treatment options, even experimental ones, but had found nothing that would actually stop the disease.

If she got it, she could take medicines,

have treatments that might slow down the course of the illness, but nothing would stop it entirely. He scrubbed at his jaw, the scrape of his beard told him he needed to shave before dinner later, but he decided to leave it for now. They were out in the woods, and what better place to do something he'd always wanted to do? Grow a beard.

Celeste wouldn't allow him to, not even a mustache, because it looked common, she'd told him more than once. He'd shaved twice a day since he was 15, at her direction, and for the first time in his life, decided to leave it. Not because he was depressed and didn't care if he looked scruffy, far from it. He felt more alive each day he spent with Marie, and being with her so often during the day now had really boosted him up. He wanted to be a little bohemian, maybe even buy a pair of carpenter's pants to go with his new coat. That had been a little bit of defiance as well, that coat.

Every time he put it on he felt that he was making a statement: I am a new man, my own man, and fuck what old women with grudges thought.

Marie liked the way his hair was cut though, so he'd leave that. He didn't know how long they'd be here, but he'd find someone down in town to do it for him. It wasn't that difficult, although the woman that usually cut it made a huge production out of what should be a ten-minute trim. They had to make you feel like you got your money's worth, he supposed.

He scanned along the perimeter, knowing that Anton would still keep an eye out in the kitchen. They would hear any vehicles that tried to make their way up to the house, but someone on foot could sneak up. Matteo doubted anyone would be out in this cold, not unless they wore Arctic clothing of some kind to keep from getting frostbite, and that had the added benefit of keeping the wearer warm for hours.

Maybe they should go to Alaska until

this was over, he thought. He wanted to take Marie to Europe next summer, so hopefully, this would all be over by then. But maybe, for now, Alaska might be more remote, safer for Marie. He wasn't sure. He wasn't even sure if she could handle more flights.

She didn't seem to realize it, but he knew when she was tired; she got this pinched look at the corner of her eyes, her lips went flat, and she rarely spoke. She'd been easily tired lately, and even now, he knew that she was probably having a nap on the couch after their epic snowball fight.

She'd be up in the night, wandering around, looking for signs that the bear had broken through the fence again, as she said when he asked. But he knew she wasn't able to get comfortable, that something was bothering her when she was in bed. She'd thrash around and make sudden movements, even when she was deeply asleep.

He went back to his computer and decided to look for other reasons she might be experiencing these problems. The first thing he found was stress. Everything was blamed on stress nowadays, something he found to be dismissive. He kept reading and found a new term - essential tremor. The site told him that essential tremors happened with movement, while tremors with Parkinson's were usually present at rest.

Well, that didn't help. He'd noticed it when she was relaxed and sitting down, and when she was reaching for something. It could be something like that, though, and while it did need to be evaluated, he wondered if perhaps she was correct and this was more of a nerve damage problem. She didn't have that pill-rolling motion that was described as a Parkinson's tremor. Maybe this wasn't such bad news.

It wasn't a discussion for today, he decided, and went back to staring at his computer. There were a lot of emails from Trina, but he'd ignored them all. He'd sent her a voice message when they left, because she hadn't answered her phone, saying that they were leaving to keep Marie safe and that he'd contact her when they could. He decided it was safe with the VPN and emailed his cousin.

She replied promptly, full of relief and wanting to join them. She knew she couldn't but wished she could. Matteo would never tell her where they were anyway. He trusted Trina, but not anyone that might be snooping in her files.

He sent another email, telling his cousin to be patient and not say anything to anyone, not even their family. He'd spread it around that he'd taken his wife to South America, but had told others that they were going to China for a trip he'd always wanted to take. Yet others heard that they'd gone to Russia.

He wasn't an expert at this hiding out thing, but he knew that if he told everyone something different that nobody would know, for sure, where to look. He couldn't stay in the office anymore after the last email and went out to join his wife, but as he suspected, she was asleep. He went into the kitchen instead and found Anton cutting up vegetables. He had beef simmering in a pot, and the smell was heavenly.

"Smells good," he told the other man and grabbed a bottle of water from the fridge.

"It'll take a few hours, but it will be worth it." Anton looked up at him with a smile, before his gaze went back to the knife cutting at vegetables expertly.

"Cool." Matteo wasn't used to being still for so long and wanted to go outside but the snow had started back up, yet again. "I'm going stir-crazy, are you?"

"A little, but I'm more used to being still for long periods of time than you are." Anton moved the carrots off the cutting board, rinsed it off, then started to chop peeled potatoes. "How is she doing?"

The question was asked in a polite tone, but Matteo knew it was momentous for the man to even ask. So, he went with honesty. "She's alright, but she's having some kind of tremor and trouble sleeping."

"Hardly surprising after the last year of her life, well, her entire life from what you've said," Anton spoke quietly. He didn't want to be overheard, not because he was judging her but because he was respecting her privacy. He didn't want her to think he was gossiping.

"I've considered that, whether it's all just stress, maybe some PTSD even, but she's worried because of her mother's history."

"I can't blame her," Anton said as he moved the potatoes away and started to cut up celery and then tomatoes. "That doesn't sound like a pleasant illness at all."

"No, and we're still keeping her a prisoner, aren't we? She can go outside now, she's not locked up in a tower, but she's still locked away here."

"Do you want to go home? Or somewhere else, maybe?" Anton began to add vegetables to the pot and stirred each new addition in slowly.

"No, I think we're fine here." Matteo scrubbed at his face again and sighed heavily. "I think I'll have to take her to a doctor in town when it stops snowing though."

"Just to ease her mind?" Anton asked after he put the lid back on the pot.

"Yes, and mine. And to an extent, yours even. We're all worried about her."

"Sounds like a good idea. Won't that register her in a system, though?" Anton pointed this out with a cringe, and Matteo understood why. What a thing to remind his boss of when he was worried about his wife.

"It probably would. Damn. We might have to take that chance. I think she's starting to get freaked out about it."

"We'll get her down there, then." Anton came to sit at the table, a cup of coffee in hand. "To ease your mind too."

"Maybe it's for the best. She needs to know. Worrying will only make it worse."

"You're right." Anton sighed and his face schooled into understanding.

"I think I'll have a nap myself. I'll be upstairs if she wakes up." Matteo stood up from the table but turned back to his employee and friend. "Thanks for everything, Anton."

"My pleasure, boss." Anton nodded and got up to check the pot as the lid began to vibrate on top of it.

Matteo went in to check on Marie before he went up to bed and saw that she was still asleep. Her dark hair fanned out behind her in a long, silky wave down her back - one of the things about her that he loved. She could cut it if she wanted to, but he knew she'd only ever have it trimmed, because she knew he liked it.

She was as generous with him as she could be, and for her, that meant she gave him every part of herself that she could. Her face was relaxed and peaceful, so he decided to leave her alone and went up to their bedroom. He slipped into a pair of pajamas and then into the bed. He found something to watch on television that looked boring enough to fall asleep to, and didn't fight the weight of his eyes.

Later that evening, he woke up and as he went down the stairs he heard Anton and Marie talking. They were laughing about a story he was telling her, something from his childhood that had her in fits of giggles. It was good to hear her laugh like that, so delighted and childlike. He knew she was happy at that moment and that was better medicine than just about anything.

He stood there for a second, thinking. He'd gone to a private school in New York and then to a prestigious university. He knew doctors all over the world, he'd contact them if it turned out Marie had Parkinson's. They'd probably know the latest treatments as several of them still contributed to scientific journals. Why hadn't he thought about that before, he wondered, but dismissed it. Stress of his own was starting to impact him.

He yawned as he started to work his way back down the stairs. It was nice to be relaxed for once, even if he was still on guard. Over the last few days, it had become obvious that they'd know if an intruder came anywhere near the house, especially after the incident with the bear. The sound of those two laughing together in the kitchen was... nice. He'd like more evenings like that.

"And what are you two in here laughing about? Was I snoring that loudly?" He walked up to the fridge to grab a bottle of wine to go with dinner and looked at the pair of them. Marie was still in a fit of giggles and Anton's face was a mixture of mirth and guilt.

"No. I told her about the time I fell down a roof I was trying to repair when I was younger, and how my pants got stuck on a nail. I hung there for hours, calling out for anyone to notice. Only nobody heard me and I was up there, dangling for hours before my pants finally tore and I plopped down into a pile of snow."

"Sounds like you were saved then. And like there was more to the story that I need to know." He pulled the cork out of the wine as Anton filled three bowls and brought them over. He went back for a basket full of hot garlic bread and brought that over too.

Anton started to retell the story to Matteo, who had never heard it, mainly because Anton just didn't talk about his childhood or anything personal really. But what Matteo paid attention to was how Anton reacted to Marie. She'd drawn him out of his shell, made him feel at home, and got him talking. She was special like that. She could draw stuff out of you and make you feel... good about yourself. It amazed him, it pleased him, and as he took a hunk of bread and dipped it into his goulash, he wondered what other amazing things she had in store for them.

# 12

"It looks like we'll be spending our anniversary indoors," Marie said to him as he came out of the office and into the living room. A long tan sectional sofa ran along the length of one wall and she was cuddled up under a blanket, staring out of the large picture window behind it. The sun was all but down now, the floodlights outside the only illumination once it disappeared completely. Anton had put the floodlights up yesterday, just to add another layer of visibility and security.

He could see large fluffy flakes falling from the gray sky above, loading onto the newly melted snow that had turned the ground sloshy the day before. Now, that layer was ice and the snow that fell on top of it would keep it that way.

"We got out yesterday for more food, at least." He joined her on the couch and put her feet in his lap. "We'll go out once the snow has cleared if you'd like to. What would you like to do?"

"Dinner and a movie," she said after some thought. "I've never been to a movie theater."

"What?" Matteo asked, surprised. "I mean, I know your mom was poor, but she never even took you to a matinee?"

"What's that?" Marie asked, her face scrunched up as she tried to think of what the word meant.

"It's an early showing of the movies at the cinema, usually during the day, on the weekends, where it's cheaper to go in." He still couldn't wrap his head around the fact that she'd never been to the movies. "You've never had buttered popcorn or nacho cheese while you sit in a room full of people with a large, overly-priced, and watered-down, huge drink of soda in a cupholder at your side?"

"No, but it sounds terrible. I've had popcorn here with you, and stuff like that back home, but not in a real theater."

"Then that's what you shall have, my love. Once the roads have cleared again."

The weather was still off and on up there, even after two more weeks in the mountains. It would be bad when the weather changed for good, he thought. They'd have to buy groceries for a month at a time instead of days or a week at a time.

If they were still up here, that is.

"You don't mind that we can't go out tonight?" he asked her, his head propped on his right arm as he looked at her.

"Not at all. I'm still spending it with you, aren't I?"

"That you are." He patted her legs and

looked at the television. She had on a documentary, something about Acadians and how they came to be in Louisiana. He watched it with her while Anton cooked in the kitchen. The man was an amazing cook and had all but taken over cooking duties from them.

At one point, Anton came in, set up two TV trays with tableware and glasses, and not long after, brought in two plates filled with lasagna and garlic bread. All freshly made. "Happy anniversary to you both. I'm going to eat, wash up, and head back up to my room once I'm done. Enjoy your evening."

"Oh, thank you, Anton," Marie said brightly with a gleam of pleasure in her eyes. "That means a lot to us."

"Thanks, man," Matteo uttered and gave his employee and friend a polite nod. "That's awfully kind of you."

"My pleasure." Anton nodded brusquely and went back towards the kitchen.

"That's just so sweet of him, to be so considerate knowing we can't go out tonight." She stuck her fork into the lasagna and moaned as she took her first bite. "That is gorgeous."

"It is," Matteo added but all he could really see was how beautiful she was as she ate. He could have been eating a cardboard box for all he knew, all he could see was Marie and the image of her as she enjoyed something as simple as her dinner.

She had liked the jewelry he bought for her and the clothes, she even had a few sweaters that she really loved, but that was because of how soft and silky the yarn felt. She took pleasure in simple things, and it always brought him back to reality. Life wasn't about how much you had, it was about how much you enjoyed the things you did have. Marie reminded him of that all the time.

He also just liked to see the pleasure on her face when she really enjoyed some thing. She was a beautiful young woman, with beautiful oval eyes and full lips, with a nose that suited her face perfectly. She definitely had an Italian look to her, but that could have been her Cajun mother as well.

"Do you know your family's history?" he asked, curiosity getting the better of him.

"You mean my ancestry?" she replied and sat back a little. Her face took on a far-away look and she looked a little troubled. "I've heard different things over the years, well, the years before my mother ran all the family off with the way she shamed us all."

"I see. What did you find out?" When she looked at him with a quirked eyebrow, he realized it all sounded a little odd. "I'm just curious about what came together to make you so beautiful."

"Ah, well, there's the Italian side. And on Mom's side: French, Spanish. There were also whispers of a quadroon mistress back in the 18th century that may have been where our line came from, and whatever else came along. They used to have these balls for slaves and free women of color that were used to place the young woman with a white man in something that wasn't considered legal marriage, but did come with a contract, usually some kind of property, and if the woman was a slave, perhaps her freedom."

"It sounds barbaric," he responded immediately.

"It does. But at the same time, the arrangement would give the young woman a home and money, something that many women did on either side of the color line, and still do to some extent." She looked down at her plate and he realized they'd both had the same thought. They'd done the same exact thing as that woman that may have been her ancestor, only their marriage was legal. She quickly got over her stumble though and carried on. "Sometimes, it was stipulated in the contract that if there were any children born from the arrangement the father would acknowledge and provide for them. Our family had money a long time ago. Mother squandered what little she was given on her dreams to be a Hollywood starlet."

"And you had nothing from it all." He pondered it all before he spoke again. "Amazing, isn't it? How things change over the generations? My family arrived poor and with barely anything to their names; my great-grandfather didn't even have a pair of shoes, but now we have enough to keep the whole family going."

"It all depends on what each of us does with what we're given, I suppose. Mom wanted to be a star and would have done anything it took to gain that dream until she knew it was over and she was out of money. She put both of us at risk, and once she knew it was over, that her dreams were dead, she gave up. She didn't care anymore. But I bet your family kept trying."

"Yes. Even without the marriage Celeste made with your father, our family was on the rise. We still are, and I'm even getting us into more legitimate businesses these days." He sat back, finished with the meal, and thought about it all. "I didn't care what I did before you came along, but I'd started to branch into less unsavory businesses. Now, I want to be above board, stay out of trouble, and be more... legitimate."

"I guess Celeste didn't care where the money came from?" She didn't like to talk about his aunt, but he didn't mind when she brought the woman up.

"No, people are things to be used, rungs to be climbed as she ascends the ladder to her own personal version of heaven. She doesn't care who or what she hurts, but she doesn't like being crossed either. That always confused me, how she could hurt without the blink of an eye, but if someone hurt her, they had to pay. As I got older, I realized it was just how selfish she was."

"That's what it sounds like to me." Marie swallowed her last bite and sat back to join him, a glass of wine in hand. "So, how are we going to spend the rest of our evening?"

"Hmm. Let me think." He pondered it for a moment, and then came up with an idea. "Sit here, I'll come to get you in a bit."

She laughed as he stood up and handed him a piece of cinnamon candy she'd pulled from a drawer. She took one and put it in her mouth with a wink. "We'll both be nice and tasty when you get back."

"Baby, you're tasty no matter what you eat." He gave her his own wink then walked away with a laugh.

A quick run through the house and he went into the bathroom. It was a little chilly, but as he lit one bag of the five bags of tea candles they had and dotted them around the bathroom, it became warmer. It was maybe a little too bright, but it wasn't so bright that it took away the romance. He started to run the bath at the temperature she liked and then went out to bring her into the bathroom with him.

"If you'll follow me please?" He held a

bottle of cold white wine in his hand and a smile on his face as she followed.

"Oh, this might be interesting," she cooed as she walked behind him. She saw two glasses for the wine and a bathtub full of bubbles. "This looks fun. Are we both going in?"

"That's the idea."

She could feel his desire radiate from his eyes, from the look on his face as she came up to him and began to undress. Her eyes were just as hungry for him and he hoped they'd at least make it into the bathtub before they started. It would be a waste to let the water go cold.

He pulled away from her before she became too enthralled with kissing him and took his own clothes off. With a moan of relief, he sank into the hot water, the instant reprieve for muscles he hadn't realized ached was almost as good as her kisses. "Come on, hop in."

She gave a rather impish little smile as she took his hand and stepped into the tub before she turned to sit in front of him. She slid between his legs and leaned back against his chest. The tub was big enough for them both and deep enough that his arms could rest easily on the sides. They both inhaled the scented steam from the bubble bath and relaxed. "This I like."

He smiled at her words. "What, are you saying there's something you don't like here?"

The question was asked with his eyes closed, the outside world far away and unable to intrude on this moment with his wife. She felt good pressed into him like that, she was totally relaxed with him now, used to being naked with him. A grin spread over his face as he thought about that first time he'd undressed her, how she'd been so shy and timid. Now, "shy and timid" wasn't the word he'd use for her at all.

Marie wouldn't argue with him on most things but that was because she tended to agree with him. If she disagreed with him, she'd usually say it. She wasn't afraid of him or his wealth, and that was a good thing. He'd wanted to dominate her, to make her his and only his, to the point where he wanted her every thought to only be of him, but he'd eased back on that when she'd started to have problems, and he saw that she did that anyway, even without his dominance.

Marie was the wife he'd always wanted, even if he hadn't known he'd wanted one. She slid down his body and turned to look at him. "What are you thinking about?"

"I'm thinking about how lucky I am." Wet fingers left a trail down her face as he ran his fingertips down her cheek.

"Are you? You're strapped with a basket-case for a wife, and now we're hiding from people that want to kill me to get back at you, how is that lucky?" The dark-brown eyes that made his heart beat with un-spoken emotions were filled with sadness, maybe even sorrow at what their lives had been like. "You had to marry me to save me from your aunt, as well."

"Ah, but I'd marry you again, Marie. Even if it wasn't to save you from Celeste. As for the hiding, I'd run across the globe if it meant you were safe." He looked down at her face and felt that emotion grow as a warmth that spread through his chest. "I'd take the world down, burn it down and rebuild it, all for you, Marie."

He smiled when her eyes went wide and her mouth fell open.

"Don't be so shocked, you've given me something I've always wanted - a home. That home lives inside of you, it is you, and I won't allow the world to take that away from me. Not again."

"I'm glad, Matteo. I'm glad you feel like that." She looked away, amazed at how he'd made her feel. "If I'm your home, it's only because you're mine."

"Then we'll burn the world down together if we have to." He pulled her up, her hot, slick skin pressed to his, and he kissed her until all thought left his head. All thoughts except for her. She filled his thoughts, his desire for her drove everything else away. The night might have been ruined by the snow, but in a way, the snow gave them the chance to have something even more special - a moment that they would always remember.

# 13

"The water is getting cold," Marie whispered to him as he rinsed her hair out.

They'd been in the tub for a while, long enough that both of them were now clean and more than a little ready to get between warm sheets. He ran his fingers over her head one last time to make sure all of the shampoo was gone before he let her up. "Okay, let's get to bed then."

They'd emptied the bottle of wine and both were just a little tipsy, but that was more being drunk on love than on the wine, she thought. He'd all but said he loved her, and she'd almost let the words slip past her lips. By now, it almost hurt to not say them, but she held them back. He wasn't ready, not yet.

The bathroom towels were large, warm, and fluffy enough to be blankets, so when she wrapped herself in one, she didn't need another. With a giggle of pure delight, she ran to their bedroom. He was right behind her.

He caught up to her and dragged her under the covers with him. The giggles turned to outright laughter. "God, I need to hear that every day."

His words jarred her and she looked at him. "Me laughing? Why?"

"Because it means you're okay, Marie, that you're still with me." He pushed the covers off their heads and pulled her to sprawl over his chest. "I could hurt you very easily, my world has already done that time after time. I don't want you to hate me for the things that come into our lives because of who I am, what I am. So, as long as you're still laughing, then I know that everything is alright."

"I see." She let her tongue flick out to wet dry lips and she saw how it caught his attention. "You do know you haven't actually hurt me, though, right?"

"I do, Marie." His voice came out gravelly, rough, as he sat up against the pillows.

Marie sat up beside him, her knees pulled up to lean against as she looked at him, the towel barely clinging together now. "I'm not with you because I have to be, Matteo, not anymore. I'm with you because I want to be."

Even if that wasn't fair to him.

Before she could let that thought fester anymore, he pulled her to him and kissed her until she was breathless, but she didn't care. She twined her tongue with his and crawled over his hips until she straddled his body. His left hand came up into the back of her hair to tilt her head to the angle he wanted, while his right came up to pull at the towel that still, somehow, clung together. He pushed it away at the same moment that he broke their kiss.

His lips teased at her nipples, sucked them into hard points before he licked them in a way that nearly had her in tears with torturous pleasure. He didn't just stop there and have his way with her. She gasped when he pushed her back swiftly, his own body moving to settle between her thighs. With a grin, she stretched her body, opened her thighs, knees up, to let him do whatever he wanted to do to her.

The sensation of soft lips against her yielding skin, his hot breath over her wet skin, then, the lap of his tongue against her folds. Her back arched to press deeper into his mouth, to find just the right spot, but he was already there. His tongue circled and flicked before he tired of teasing her.

The drum of his tongue against her clit matched the race of blood in her veins. Something welled up in her, words that she wanted to scream, but she held those words back and panted his name instead. Softly, over and over, she said his name as he continued to drive her higher.

She thought she'd lose her mind when he slid two fingers into her hot center, when she felt him reach that spot that so many called a myth. They were people that didn't know, that didn't know that Matteo was a miracle worker who had found it, and knew exactly how to work it.

The world exploded around her, it must have, because all the oxygen left her body and she shook, trembled, convulsed through something that was pleasurable, that stole everything from her, and made the world stop for long seconds. It all went blank, and then, with a cry of shock, it all came over her again. She thought she'd pass out. She needed air but then didn't care if she ever breathed again because Matteo had her in his arms. His tongue drove her high, over and over.

In an instant, he was gone. His tongue left her and his fingers exited the heated cocoon they'd filled, and she felt deprived.

She held her hands out to him, but instead of taking her hands, he pulled her to the end of the bed by her ankles and flipped her over. She slid down to the floor and leaned over the bed, knowing what he wanted.

She flicked her hair until it trailed down her back, a tease in itself. She liked it when he pulled her hair, and he took her up on the invitation, the suggestion. He wrapped his right hand in the long strands until her head pulled back just as he thrust into her.

This time she moaned his name louder, unable to hide the sob of desire in her voice. Another shudder went through her as his left hand found its home on her hip, tilted them just the right way before it moved to smooth down her back, to direct her into the perfect arch that would allow him to sink deeper into her.

He tugged at her hair again as he began to move inside of her. His other hand brushed against the curve of her ass, before his palm landed on the rounded flesh, a sharp pain that began to burn in a way that she found shockingly thrilling.

"Don't come, Marie, not yet," he directed her. She tried, she really did, but that first warning of a pulse that had told him she was about to, was something she couldn't control, not anymore. She'd tried, but she hadn't mastered it.

He stopped, coming to a standstill until she found her breath, until she found that control that had slipped. But her concentration was still on him, on the way he felt inside of her. She felt her walls quiver around him, demanding to be stroked by his thick cock. But he didn't move, not until he heard her take a deep breath.

He rocked into her gently at first, to build her back up slowly, to give himself time to enjoy the sensation of her wrapped around him. "Fuck, you feel so good, Marie."

The words were ragged, as if he hadn't wanted to say them, but couldn't help it. That sent a shiver up her spine and a surge through her walls that already felt like they'd turned to liquid silk.

She smelled him on every inch of her body, felt him, and her fingers clutched in the covers as she tried not to scream. She wanted to come, she was so close. If he'd just speed up a little bit, just a little more, that's all she needed. A little.

She squeezed her already tight walls until they clamped around him, and he gave the expected grunt of pleasure mixed with surprise. His hand, still wrapped in her hair, pulled a little more and the sting of pain that gave her set her off all over again. "I can't help it, Matteo. Please, come with me. Come with me, baby."

She panted it all out, in time with the quick, deep thrusts he gave her now. His hand let loose of her hair so that he could grasp both sides of her hips with his fingers. The tips dug in, painfully, but it turned to pleasure in her brain as he drove harder, drove her into another wave of pulses that left her unable to think.

They clung together, still joined as they caught their breath. He finally slid up onto the bed, then pulled her up beside him. She was still lost in the bliss of being utterly satisfied, her eyes closed against anything that might make the sensation end. She needed that moment like she would need a drug; it was her drug now, given to her only by Matteo.

She curled into his side and listened to him as he began to snore softly. A smile spread over her face as she realized he'd fallen asleep quickly. Turning away, she pulled her left leg up to rest against the bed while her right leg stayed straight. Her legs felt restless, though, so she moved them around until she figured out nowhere was comfortable. It was one of the things keeping her up at night now, her legs just felt so very… restless.

She reached for a robe and slipped the long light green fleece over skin now covered in goosebumps. Even with the fires, the air was still cool if you weren't clothed.

Padding softly to the window, Marie opened the curtain just enough to look out. There was even more snow on the ground now, and it continued to fall. The floodlights lit up the night, which was supposed to help discourage the bear from coming back, or so Anton had told her.

She knew it was just to make sure they could see more of the area around the house. In the distance, she could see the dark line of trees that clung to the hills and mountains around here. Cedar, pine, and a few other kinds of trees populated the mountain the house was built on. Snow covered them all now, turned them into blobs that could be anything.

Marie wondered how many nights she'd spend like this, unable to sleep but so tired. Even when she made up for her lack of sleep with a nap, she felt tired the next day, like she'd never feel rested ever again. She knew it, she knew it in her bones, even without seeing a doctor - she was doomed.

A snuffle from the bed drew her attention and again she wondered if she should just run away. He didn't deserve the hell that was coming. He didn't deserve to sit and watch her wither away. Or spend all of his money trying to make her well again.

She turned back to the window, pain a tight vice around her heart. She didn't want to leave him. He'd said only a few hours ago that she was his home. But he hadn't seen the end stages of Parkinson's disease. He didn't know the shame of losing control of your own body, of how you became totally, completely dependent on someone to take care of you.

That frightened her, and she wasn't sure she wanted to keep living if she made it to that point, if it became that bad for her. Her mother had even started to lose the ability to speak towards the end, to swallow. That was no way to live, was it?

For a moment, for a very brief moment, she understood some of her mother's anger. She'd been helpless and that was one thing Ruby hated above everything. Marie hoped she didn't turn out like that, but she knew it was unlikely. Her mother had been a terror before she became ill; she'd been mean and cruel before the first signs appeared.

No, she wouldn't end up being an abusive bitch, but would she become depressed, unresponsive? Would she give up?

They were all questions she'd thought about a thousand times, but each night, when she couldn't get to sleep, or back to sleep if she'd been asleep, they came back to haunt her. They made her question whether it was fair to stay with Matteo, to let him become even more attached to her.

Maybe she should just go away, disappear, but where would she go? All she had left was the house in Louisiana. Could she go back there? She missed the quiet of the house, the way the night sprang into life with the sounds of insects and animals on the prowl. The noise in New York, that constant noisy hum, was something she'd become accustomed to, but now that she'd thought about it, she thought maybe it was time to go home. Back to where life made sense.

Motion caught her attention and she became still, breath held, as she stared into the space where the light faded into darkness. Was it the bear, back to scratch its back and explore the place where the humans had invaded? She narrowed her eyes to try to focus in on the spot, but it didn't happen again. It was probably just a raccoon then, she decided, and left the bedroom to make a cup of chamomile tea.

The tea soothed her but it never helped her get back to sleep. It was pleasant though, and she sipped at it while she flicked through a list of stories on different channels on YouTube. She'd found a few people that read out stories in a variety of genres, and she liked to listen to them when she needed to sleep. It was enough to distract her brain and help her get to sleep sometimes.

She'd grown up in a household where most technologies were something she saw on television or outside of the home. She'd had some things from school, but they'd never been hers, it was just stuff for school. After that, there'd been no money to pay for fancy smartphones or computers. Internet would have been another bill she would have had to pay, so she'd done without it.

Now, she was discovering there were things she could do that she could have never dreamed about doing. It was amazing, but right now, she just wanted to sleep. It would be nice to not have to walk around like a zombie, trying to function with zero energy.

She listened to the story as it played until everything faded into black. Sleep came at last, and when Anton gently draped a blanket over her, she didn't feel it. She also wasn't aware of how he stood guard at the windows, watching the darkness, because he'd seen that slight movement as well. He wasn't certain it was trouble, but his job was to protect her now, for Matteo. He would not slack in his duty.

The poor woman had been through enough and he felt for her. He watched until the sun came up and Matteo came down to start breakfast. Anton held a finger to his lips when he spotted his boss, and Matteo nodded.

They both went into the kitchen and spoke softly.

"How long has she been down here?" Matteo asked, sleep still a hoarseness in his voice.

"All night, but she slept through it. I saw something outside, then heard her moving around, so I came down to watch over her." The big man's voice was quiet, gentle, as he watched his boss put the coffee on and take the bacon out of the fridge.

"Thanks, Anton. Go up and get some sleep, if you want. Or do you want to eat first?"

"I'll eat, yeah. Then, I might get some sleep, thanks."

When Marie woke up, it was to the smell of bacon and coffee. Stretching, she smiled. She'd slept all night and someone had put a blanket over her.

When she walked into the kitchen, she saw a tired-looking Anton and a rested Matteo. It must have been the big man that had put the blanket over her. She gave him a grateful nod and then hugged her husband. "Hi, there."

He put a kiss on her forehead and squeezed her softly before he motioned to the table. "Get some coffee and have a seat. Food's almost ready."

With a clear head and a rested body, Marie watched her husband as he hummed along to the radio, cooking pancakes to go with the bacon. How could she change that bright and happy face to one of exhaustion and worry? It just wouldn't be fair. She plastered on a smile and decided to wait. She had to think about this more, but for now, she couldn't resist his happiness. Later, she decided. She'd think about it all again later.

# 14

"The road is clear, although you might find there are some patches of black ice now that the sun has gone down." Anton sat on the couch in the living room, ready for a night on his own with a few beers, a boxing match ready to start, and some snacks.

"Thanks, Anton," Matteo said and took the keys to the SUV from the coffee table. "We'll be back around 11 or 12, not sure. It depends on what she wants to do after we go to the movies."

"Sure, I'll keep a watch on everything here." Anton picked up a bag of corn chips and opened them. He'd been down to the town earlier to get food and other necessities while the weather was clear.

Matteo and Marie were on their way out to dinner and a movie, and his wife was nearly dancing with excitement. She was dressed in a thick black sweater, black leggings, with her black wool coat on over that. She even had a black knit cap on her head. "You look like a burglar."

"What?" she asked, her eyes wide with dismay. "Do I?"

"A little, but it's sexy. Come on, my little thief, let's get out of here before the weather changes its mind again." Matteo had learned it was possible up here, but it shouldn't get too bad in the couple of hours they were down in town. If it did, he'd rent them a room at the local hotel and they'd stay there until the weather improved. Not a big deal really.

They went out to the SUV and were on their way down the mountain.

"I'm so excited."

"I can tell." He laughed softly as he drove expertly down the steep incline. "I still can't believe you've never been to the movies."

"There wasn't any money and nobody to take me." She repeated something she'd said before, but not with self-pity, she was simply stating a fact.

"What else haven't you done?" he pondered out loud. He glanced at her swiftly before he put his eyes back on the road. "Have you been to a fair, to a prom? Or a club? Have you ever been to any of those?"

"No, no, no, and no. I think." She laughed as she answered, amused at how shocked he was. "I lived under a rock, remember? Well, a roof that I barely left. I'd have to travel to Baton Rouge or New Orleans sometimes, maybe down to Houma or over to Sorrento. But I've never been so far as I have since I met you. I never went to any of the festivals or fairs, even church fairs. Our church used to have a couple in the spring and summer, just to raise funds

for activities with the younger con-
gregation."

"And then your mother was excommu-
nicated. That must have been tough on you,
to lose the church community." He spoke
gently, as if afraid to bring up a sore subject.

"She was, but I wasn't. I stopped going
though, it was too far to walk and she
wouldn't drive me. By the time I was able to
drive, I'd lost interest." Her voice wasn't bitter, but he saw a tightness around her eyes
that she quickly wiped away. "They didn't
help me. They knew what I was living with,
but none of them helped."

"There must have been a lot of people
that looked the other way. I don't know
how social services didn't become involved." He didn't want to upset her, but
he'd wondered about it often. Why had the
state left her there with that horrible
woman that had been her mother?

"CPS was called quite often, so maybe
some of them did try to help. I was on a
first name basis with many of the social

workers, but they couldn't prove I was abused or neglected. I was too afraid of my mother's wrath to tell them the truth when they came or demanded my mother bring me in. I'd make sure she was sober, fed, and had taken a bath, all the things she'd forget to do, on the days when the social workers came to inspect the house or when she had to take me to them. I was the one that cleaned up her messes, which kept everything tidy. I learned how to use the washer when I was five so I'd have clean clothes for school." She took a deep breath, then let it out slowly. "It's weird. I'm angry at people for not helping, but I'd lie to the social services people when they came around."

"What has your counselor said?" He knew she'd stopped talking to the counselor when they came out to Montana, but she'd kept up a dialogue while they were still in New York, at least online.

"That I was a child. I did what I had to to survive. That I'd probably go through a lot of emotions as time goes by. The five stages of grief and all that."

"Five stages of grief?" he asked, not sure what that was.

"Yes. I'm not sure who invented it or whatever, but it's a model of how people deal with grief, usually when they've lost a loved one or have been given a terminal diagnosis. Or they've had a life like mine."

"Okay, so what are these stages?"

"Denial, anger, bargaining, depression, and acceptance." She paused, her lips twisted to the left as she thought about it. "I think it's more that I'm all over the place at the moment. A lot has happened, hasn't it?"

"It has. And I'm sorry I've only added to the weight you carry, Marie." He took her hand as they came to a stop sign at the bottom of the mountain. "I'm so sorry."

"You don't have to be, you got me out of that, you know? It's because of you I can start to deal with all of this; I can grieve, I can heal." She paused, as if she wanted to say something more, then changed her mind. "You've given me the world, Matteo, and I'm glad I get to have all these 'first times' with you."

"I hope you don't come to regret it, at some point," he started, but then let her go on when she started to speak. He pulled out onto the road into town and listened to her.

"I think I'm in the anger stage right now. I denied a lot of what I thought and felt, what I experienced. I told myself it was all normal, that I deserved it, even if I sometimes hated my mother. Now, I'm just angry at all of them: her for making me lie, them for not demanding answers from her. I'm angry that it all happened to a child, that a child had to go through that."

"I guess I was lucky, wasn't I?" he whispered, but she heard him.

"Were you?" she asked with a pointed look. "Celeste doesn't sound like she was much better."

"Does that mean I'm still in denial?" He tried to laugh it off, but she looked away as if she was trying to hold something back. "I had everything I wanted: all the toys, the cars, the clothes, I was allowed to go out…"

"But were you given love, Matteo?" she interrupted and he could hear the anger in her voice now. "Celeste gave you items, belongings, but she denied you *love*. She was cruel to you. Was that any better than what my mother did?"

She was breathing hard and her cheeks were flushed. He didn't realize she cared so much. Maybe because nobody ever had before, not like Marie did. It was hard to recognize now.

"I suppose you have a point." He sat back, his focus on driving but his thoughts racing. "Yeah, I see your point."

"I'm sorry you had it so rough, Matteo. I want to make that all better for you," she said and he could hear the emotion that strangled her voice. "I don't want to make it worse."

"You could never do that, Marie." He pulled into the restaurant they had a reservation at and parked up. With a quick move, he turned to her, took her face in his hands, and looked into her eyes. His eyes were so full of emotion they almost glowed as he stared at her intently. "You are my home, remember?"

"I remember," she whispered with a watery smile. "And you're mine."

She clutched at the necklace he'd given her and her smile strengthened. "Okay, this was supposed to be a fun, carefree night. Let's stop being grownups now and play a little bit."

"I think that sounds like the best idea I've heard in a long time. Let's go."

The dinner went well and before long, they were standing in line to get popcorn and drinks at the snack counter of the theater. Matteo watched her as she looked around.

"Oh my, they have hotdogs, and all that candy..." Her voice trailed off as she looked at the rows and rows of overpriced candy. "It's so amazing."

"It is nice, the whole experience," he

agreed, but the charm had worn off for him a long time ago. "I'm looking forward to the movie, it looks like it's going to be good in the trailers."

"Let's hope it's not one of those where they show the best parts in the trailer and the rest is terrible," she laughed as they moved up the line.

Before long, they were settled into their seats and he watched as she gazed around the room they were in. "There are so many people."

She whispered it to him, so he whispered back. "Hopefully they've turned their phones off."

"I hope so."

The movie started then, and thankfully, the room went quiet. Matteo wanted to watch the movie, but his mind was on other things. She'd missed out on so much. She'd basically been her mother's prisoner. The only times she'd gone out was to go to school, to go to meetings with social services, and then later, to go on errands for her mother.

Matteo knew how her mother had treated her. She'd opened up to him about some of the things her mother used to tell her, he'd heard it once. Ruby had made Marie her prisoner, her slave, and though he hadn't made her a slave, he was keeping her prisoner. She was alive right now, as she watched the movie and absently shoved popcorn into her mouth. She was experiencing something he'd come to take for granted.

He'd denied her the chance to go out and do the things she'd wanted. Yeah, he'd done it to keep her safe, but was that any better than what her mother had done to her? He sighed deeply and she turned to him with a quirked eyebrow. He smiled in answer and took her hand.

For a moment, he remembered being a child and how he'd loved to go to the Sunday matinee with his real mother before Celeste took him away. His real mother was someone he rarely thought about now. He'd loved her dearly when he was little and had only wanted to go home to her once Celeste took him. But over the years, after many, many punishments, he'd learned to stop asking for her.

She'd become an alcoholic over time. She'd learned to hide her pain behind a haze of alcohol. It had allowed her to bury the guilt over letting Celeste take him, of being weak and powerless. He knew he should try to rebuild a relationship with her, to heal the wound it had left in him, but he felt like Marie was healing all of that. Maybe one day, when this was all over and Celeste was no longer a problem, he could go and see her.

And maybe he'd take Marie back to New York. Hiding out here made keeping her safe much easier, but was it really what she needed? She'd said it so many times now, but he hadn't heard her. She needed to breathe, to be free, to experience life. She was safe here, but was she alive?

He put his arm around her, and she cuddled closer to him. The ecstatic smile she wore made his heart melt. "Can we stay for another one?"

"If I wasn't worried about snow, I'd say yes. But we need to head back once it's finished."

"I understand." She leaned over to kiss him and went back to watching the movie.

Yeah, maybe it would be best to take her back. She needed to talk to her counselor some more, and he knew she wanted to see her doctor. She was worried, and he had to admit, he was concerned about the tremors, the restless nights she had, and maybe a doctor's assurance would help. That had to be weighing her mind down too, worrying that she was going to end up like her mother.

Well, she could never be like her mother. She wasn't made from the same cloth, even if they did share genes. Marie would overcome anything that came her way, she always had before. She'd get through this too. He'd be there every step of the way.

He decided to talk to Anton and see what he thought. If they could keep her safe in New York, he'd take her back to the city and let her run wild if she wanted to.

## 15

When they got home Matteo kissed Marie and headed into the kitchen to talk to Anton. She wasn't sure what it was about, but they often had these little talks, so she went up to the bathroom to shower before bed. He'd been acting strange since they left the theater, lost in his own thoughts.

She thought, perhaps, their discussion before they'd arrived for dinner had set him to thinking. Her goal hadn't been to depress him or make him feel sorry for her, she hadn't even had a goal. He'd asked questions and she'd answered as best she could.

She wanted to share with him, and he'd even done a bit of sharing of his own.

There was no use worrying over it, so she showered, put on some warm pajamas, and went to bed. He came up after a while and she asked him if he wanted to watch something.

"Yeah, find something funny. I'd like to end the night laughing with you." He winked at her before he went to the bathroom.

She found a new comedy on Netflix and had everything ready for him when he came back in.

"I went down and got you a bottle of water and some apple juice." He held both bottles up and she took them with a grateful smile.

"I'll be up all night if I drink both of those." She put them on a napkin she'd put there to protect the nightstand from moisture.

"I wasn't sure which you'd want. I'll take the one you don't want."

She handed over the apple juice and opened the water. He settled into bed and pulled her to him, with his arm over her shoulders. "What are we watching then?"

She told him the plot of the movie. He seemed to like it, so she put it on. She stayed awake for the first hour, but by the time the movie was almost done she was almost asleep. She had turned over, onto her right side away from him, because she just couldn't keep her eyes open anymore.

"Marie?" he asked quietly, as if afraid to wake her but needing to talk to her.

"What, babe?" She reached back and took his hand in hers.

"Do you want to go back to New York?" The question came just as quietly but she heard him.

"What?" She rolled over, awake now. "Back to New York? But there's still someone after me, isn't there?"

"I talked with Anton. We can work out a way to keep you protected there: keep guards with you, change routes when you go somewhere, keep security tight. It will be a challenge, but if you want to go home, we can." He turned to her and she touched his face, a little rough now at the end of the night.

He'd shave it all away in the morning. She thought about those few days he'd let it grow before he'd had to shave it off because it itched him so much. "You know my home is you, remember?"

"I do, I meant it too. But you've been a prisoner your whole life, Marie. First your mother's, then mine when this contract was made. I've done it to keep you safe, but it's not much different is it?" His eyes searched hers, begged her to tell him he was wrong, and she could only smile.

"At first, I felt the same, I have to admit. I wanted to escape the seclusion, the in-ability to breathe fresh air. I knew why it had to be like that, Matteo. I knew this was my life that was in danger. You didn't keep me at the house to be your maid, to throw things at me, to make me wipe your ass, or change sheets you'd pissed in, on purpose I might add. She did that so many fucking times."

Marie started to swear as she spoke more about her mother. She didn't always swear, but when she did, it was usually because she was talking about her mom, or very upset about something. Some emotion prodded her into it, and she knew there must be anger showing through on her face. She tried to calm herself down, to relax as he waited for her to continue.

He needed to be reassured that she didn't hate him, and she didn't. She cupped his cheek in her palm, slid a finger over his lips, and looked straight into those gray eyes that made her melt now, as they always did.

"You didn't keep me there to degrade me, Matteo. You kept me there, you brought me here, to keep me safe. It's totally different." A tear slid from her eye, but she wasn't sure why. Maybe it was the sensation of loving him that made the tears come to her eyes, she wasn't sure, because she wasn't sad, just... in love. "You have been nothing but wonderful to me."

"But I've brought my world to you. I've brought the shit that comes with it. With me. If it wasn't for me, you'd be safe right now."

"Would I? Or would I be homeless, wondering when I would be able to eat next, where I'd sleep?" She smiled, a sad smile, but one that changed as she looked at him. Hope took the place of sadness. "You saved me, Matteo, and you gave me the world."

"Maybe I should take you away from all of that forever," he mused as he rolled to his back.

"What? And give up your life there? What you've become after all those years of hard work?"

"For you? I just might, Marie. I've been thinking about it. I'm independently wealthy. My money doesn't come from family money. I learned a long time ago that Celeste was looking out for herself, even if she tried to give the illusion that it was all for the family." His fingers ran over the tattoo on his right arm, the one that ran up from his wrist, up to the point where it became a crown on that side of his chest. "I keep my family in money, but any of them could do that, Trina could."

He paused, brought his fingers to her face to tilt it back up to him. "I would give it all up for you, Marie. Every bit of it, even my own wealth. We could go buy a farm in Nebraska, or here if you want to. Have babies and cows while we grow wheat or whatever they grow out here. We could disappear, be whoever we wanted to be."

She smiled, the idea exciting, but the smile faded. "I think we should go back. Let me go to the doctor, find out if this tremor is just PTSD or some trapped nerve, or whatever before we make any radical decisions."

"Ah, right, yeah. You're right." He took a deep breath through his nose and smiled. "Anyway, shall I turn this movie off and convince you why I'm the only man you'll ever need?"

"Oh, I think you've proven that already, Matteo, time and time again. But I could take a little more convincing." She grinned and took his face in her hands as she crawled over him. "I'll never get enough of your convincing."

"That's why you're my woman, Marie. Always so eager for my touch." He breathed the words up at her, intense and growly. "Always so ready for me and only me."

"And here I thought it was just my looks." She brought his hands up to her breasts as she sat up. "And these."

"Oh, definitely those too." He grinned as he squeezed her nipples in just the right way, through her pajamas. "So many reasons, really. All of them make you mine."

He growled it out, and she felt something go quivery and tight deep inside. Fuck, he made her hot with just his words, she thought. With another growl, he pulled her back to his face and silenced them both with a kiss that she was certain melted her forever.

SHE WAS UP AGAIN hours later, her legs once again telling her that she needed to walk, walk, walk, but she was too tired to walk. Another cup of chamomile tea and she went back to the window in the living room. Great, more snow. She blew air out of her nose and walked to the couch.

Something, some noise, made her head whip back to the window. What was that?

She opened the curtains a notch and looked out. There was movement over by the trees again, but then it stopped. She heard footsteps on the stairs and turned to see Anton coming down.

"I'll go check, see what it was. You stay in here."

"Should I wake Matteo?" she asked him when she saw the worry on his face.

"No, it's probably just raccoons at the

SUMMER COOPER

trash bin. I forgot to take it down when I went into town earlier. I'll be back in a few." He gave her a nod and then went to the door.

She went back to watching out of the window. She saw the big man walk over to the place where they stored the household garbage, and then walk away. The snow was falling really hard now, but he seemed to be fine out there. He walked over to the trees and looked around some more. Before long, he walked back to the house and came in.

"I'll put some hot water on, or do you want coffee? You must be cold." He hadn't even put a coat on before he'd walked outside.

"Hot chocolate sounds good." He nodded, his typical response, and turned away towards the woodstove, but she'd seen the red in his cheeks.

She made the drink and brought it over to him.

"Did you see anything?"

"That snow is falling hard, so I didn't see

any tracks, but the lid to the bin was off. I'm guessing the noise scared whatever it was off. Raccoons, probably."

"Probably. I didn't see anything that looked like a man." She walked back to the table where she'd put down her chamomile tea.

"You saw it?" He looked surprised.

"Well, I heard something, then went back to the window. I didn't see anything clearly, but I saw something scurrying away. It could have been anything, I guess." She shrugged and looked back at him. "Probably raccoons, like you said."

"I think it probably was." He took a drink from his mug and turned to face the stove. "You alright down here? I can stay with you. Ahem, if you want."

He sounded so nervous, so very shy, that she wanted to laugh because it was so cute, but she held it back. She'd never met a man like Anton. She'd seen him talk to other women just fine, but she made him nervous. He was like a teenaged boy that had never spoken to his boss's wife before, even after all this time. That was probably because Matteo was asleep, she thought, and sat down.

"I'll be fine down here, you can go back up if you want, or stay here, whichever you want to do. I'm just going to put a story on and try to get to sleep."

"Why don't you try it in bed with headphones?" He turned back around, his head down, but she saw his cheeks turn redder.

"The headphones hurt my ears if I fall asleep with them in, so I come down here, so I won't disturb Matteo."

"I see. Alright, well, I'll let you get back to it then." He put his cup in the sink and started to leave the kitchen. "Sleep well."

"Thanks, you too." She gave him a little wave as he left and she went back into the living room, amused with him. He used to frighten her because he looked so grim, but then she figured out he was just really shy. He wasn't as scary as that guy Matteo had down in New Orleans; now that guy gave her the creeps, whatever his name was. She couldn't remember it now, but she could remember his face. Scary fucker.

She sipped at her tea as she browsed for a story, and smiled when she found one full of dragons, knights, and princes. Matteo was her prince, her king, really. He even had the crown on his chest to prove it. She pulled a blanket over herself, adjusted the cushions just right, and started to listen to the story.

It wasn't working yet, she realized after a while. By now, she was at least tuning in and out as sleep settled over her. She'd listened to at least a half-hour of the two-hour-long story, but she was still awake.

It wasn't her legs that kept her awake now, though. It was that noise. Would raccoons come back two nights in a row? And how was it getting in? She'd suggest a walk around the perimeter tomorrow, she decided. If they stayed. Matteo had asked her if she wanted to go home, back to New York.

She wasn't sure she did. She missed Trina, she missed the convenience, but did she miss the place? Not really, she decided after some thought. The story played on, but she let it, in the hopes that it would re-capture her imagination and send her to sleep.

This was a big decision, huge. She'd be in more danger, but she'd be able to go out. Was that what she wanted? Matteo would worry himself to death if they went back, but at the same time, he'd have a crew of people around her all the time. She'd look like some celebrity with bodyguards, trying to walk around the malls or go for lunch.

She tried to picture Trina's reaction to that and had to laugh. The other woman would glare, give them the finger, and talk about her period or something, just to make them wish they'd chosen another career. Trina liked to shock people, especially people that she didn't like. She wouldn't like the guards because she would see them as intrusive.

It would be funny though.

She stretched her legs out on the couch and tried to refocus on the story. Her ears weren't listening to it though, they were listening for noise outside. Whatever it was, raccoon or not, it had spooked her. Suddenly, she didn't feel safe on her own downstairs, and with a gasp, she got up and ran to the bedroom. She'd open a book and read herself to sleep if she had to, but she didn't want to be downstairs on her own anymore.

She wrapped herself in blankets and the warmth of Matteo's reassuring presence. She was sure it was just an animal outside, but just in case, she wanted to be with Matteo. That was the only place she truly felt safe.

# 16

---

"What about Europe?" Matteo asked as they had lunch the next day. Toasted cheese sandwiches and tomato soup, one of her favorites. "You have a passport now. Or South America?"

"I don't know," she said as she wiped her mouth to make sure she didn't have any crumbs on her face. "I've never thought about going that far away. I'd barely even thought about leaving Louisiana until you came along."

"I want to show you everything, the entire world." He smiled and she wondered if he was thinking about all the places they could go.

"I do have one request." She looked away, a little embarrassed. It wasn't the typical way people wanted to travel, but it had been a dream of hers for a while. "I always wanted to just buy a van or an RV, something I could drive around, sleep in, and use as my home. It wouldn't have to be fancy: just something with a shower, a small kitchen, and a place to sleep."

"That sounds nice actually." Matteo nodded and looked back at her. "We'll talk about it some more later. I have to make a phone call. I really need to get back soon, but I like having you to myself out here, I have to admit. And not just because I know you're safe, but because we get to do this."

"It has been nice," she agreed and stood to clear the table. Anton was asleep, he'd been up all night, so it had just been Matteo and her for lunch.

"If we go back and stay in New York, I'll have to make a point of keeping my lunches clear for you. And make more time for you, as well." He said it like it was a promise, but Marie knew he'd be busy if they went back to that life.

She turned the radio on as she cleaned up and tried to decide what to have for dinner. She took out a few things, poured herself a glass of juice, and sat down with a pad of paper, a pen, and an old atlas she'd found in a drawer in the living room. She started to list off the places she'd like to go and see.

By the time Matteo came back in, she had quite a long list of places to visit. If they started in New York, they could head straight down to Florida, then all the way across to California. From there, it would be up to Canada, or maybe down to Mexico, and all the places there were to see down there.

"If we rent one of those tour buses, you know, like famous people have? Okay, one of those, we'd have a bedroom, a bathroom, even a washer, and dryer, along with a kitchen. Or we could buy one." Her excitement made her talk fast and her cheeks were flushed.

He looked at her and she could see he was fascinated. "What have you been doing?"

"Planning out where I'd like to go." She handed over the pad of paper to him and watched as he read all of the places.

"This would take a long time," he noted and looked up at her with his eyebrows drawn together. "Do you want to live like this for months, maybe years?"

"If we can, sure. I don't need a fancy penthouse and lots of clothes, Matteo. You gave me all of that and I love it, don't get me wrong, but I'm a simple girl, I like simple things. I don't need to be..." she paused to try to find the right word, "fancy, I guess. I don't need that. I need you and if that means we stay put in New York, or we become nomads, as long as I'm with you..."

She let the words trail off because she wasn't certain he wanted to do it now. He seemed hesitant, and she didn't want to push him into something he didn't want. As long as she was with him, she didn't care anyway.

"I'm not trying to discourage you. I just want to know what you want, that you're sure it's what you want?" He sat down beside her and looked at her with seeking eyes.

"I'd love this, actually. If it hadn't been for you, I'd be homeless, living in that car of mine. My plan was to travel until I found a place to call home, once my mom passed. I knew it would happen eventually, and that was my plan. Sell everything and just find a new home. Then you came along." She shrugged and left off the part where she'd had to marry him to save everything, even herself.

It wasn't a sore spot anymore, but she didn't think it needed mentioning again. She'd come to terms with it, they both had, and had found they'd got far more out of the marriage than they'd ever dreamed of.

There was no need to throw it out there at him.

"So, you really do want to travel?" He picked the pad of paper back up again and looked it over. "I could buy us something nice, put Anton in charge, and maybe Trina, she's a smart girl. She wants to have something more to do anyway. This might be possible."

She squealed happily and leaned over to hug him. "Oh, I hope we can do this. It would be amazing, I swear. We could start in New York and go in any direction you wanted to go to. We could even go up to Canada if we wait until spring. The roads will be better. No snow."

"Hmm, maybe we should buy one in Florida. Fly down and go across and down until the warmer months hit, then go up." He showed her a new path and she nodded in agreement.

"That sounds good too. Oh, and I looked it up, we can get wifi in most of the places we'd park up, and if not, we can buy a mobile device to plug into a laptop or something. I don't know the specifics of it yet, but I know we can do that. And there's cell service too, so we don't have to be completely out of touch. You can check in with whoever you leave in charge if that's what you want to do."

He looked over at her, amazed at all the information she'd gathered so quickly. "This is really what you want to do? I know I keep asking, but I want you to be sure."

"For a while, I wanted to take over the family business, your job, but then, well, I don't think I'm ever going to be that tough, that hard, that I can do what you do." She looked down at her nails and twisted her lips into a frown. "If you want to stay and run the empire, Matteo, I understand. But, if you want to do this, then I'm all in like I said. Don't do this just for me. I don't want you to hate me for walking away, or leaving it for a while."

"I won't." He assured her with his palm

against her cheek. "I'd give it all up for you, baby."

"But you don't have to. We can find a way to make this work, I know we can." Her eyes implored him to agree to it, and she could see he was pulled to agree. His eyes flicked to the list of places and she laughed with happiness when he nodded.

"I'll start looking for a bus, RV, whatever it is that will be suitable. We have to remember though, Marie, there is a contract out on you."

"Still no word on who put it out?" She hadn't asked him a lot about it, but she'd heard him talking about it with Anton.

"No, and it's really starting to piss me off. I have a list of suspects, but I can't prove who it is. It's usually not that hard to find out, but this time, it's like finding a ghost. Usually, whoever put it out would declare it proudly, but not this time, and that makes me wonder." He cut the words off and turned his face away.

With narrowed eyes, Marie stared at

Matteo. "Do you think it's Celeste? The way she was that day she came to see me…"

"She came to see you? Why didn't you tell me?" His head whipped back around to face her, his face angry for a moment, but then it smoothed out. "Sorry, when was that?"

"Right before she left and everything kind of turned into chaos, and I wasn't well, so I forgot to tell you. I think I pissed her off." She frowned and looked at her nails again. "I might have implied she was a little too consumed with your private life."

"You wouldn't be wrong about that," he chuckled and sat back. "What else happened?"

"Not a lot. She came in, asked if you were there, then asked if we could call a truce. I agreed, for your sake, then she commenced to insulting me. Kept talking about how she'd raised you to think with your brain and not your dick, and how you only wanted me in your bed, and the minute I got too old you'd replace me.

Which is why I asked her if she was jealous."

The memories were clear in her mind and Marie could still picture Celeste's shock when the question was asked if Matteo's aunt was jealous that Marie was in his bed.

"Oh, dear. Brave of you to give as good as you got, but yeah, you baited a tiger there." He stroked his jaw and she could hear the bristle of his beard. He hadn't shaved that morning, which she found kind of sexy, but the prickle of it against her skin could be a little painful. He'd shave when he felt like it. "What else?"

"She said she didn't like me, didn't think I was the wife you deserved. And that if she didn't get rid of me, you would when you grew tired of me." The words came out more slowly as she thought about the implication. If she didn't get rid of Marie. What lengths would she go to in order to accomplish that?

"Hm. Anything else?" He waited for her answer, his face lined with concern.

"Not much. She said she hoped we wouldn't meet again and left."

"Right." He clasped his hands together and brought his index fingers up to his lips. "Hm."

"What? Do you think it's her?" Marie turned her whole body to face him, her feet on the wrung beneath his seat. "Is she the one that put the contract out?"

"I'm not sure. Maybe. I need to talk to Anton." He inhaled deeply and a dark cloud passed over his face, a look that was a mix of hurt, anger, and confusion. "Fuck."

"I'm sorry baby. It's just, at first I was so angry I couldn't think straight. And there was so much going on. I wanted to forget it, to just be with you and wipe things like her and my mother out of my mind. Because that's what it was like, listening to my mother all over again. Only, I didn't back down, as I would so often with my mother." She shuddered and looked out at the snow on the ground. It was so bright outside that she'd thought about drawing the curtains but had left them alone. She liked being able to see outside.

She hadn't let this whole contract business worry her, she felt safe out here and might have even forgotten about it if Anton and Matteo weren't always talking about security. Now, though, she had to face it.

"It's not your fault, Marie," he answered and took her hands in between his. "You were under a lot of stress, and then the attack happened, you aren't to blame."

"No, but maybe I should have told you earlier." She shrugged yet again and met his eyes. "If it's her, what can be done?"

"I'm not sure. She wasn't one of my favorite people before you came along. Now? I'll do what I have to." He pulled away from her, stood up, and walked over to the fridge.

She knew he needed that distance from her, to not touch her because he never wanted her to be near anything he considered dirty. If the expression on his face told her anything, it told her that he was thinking very bad things. Things he wouldn't want her to know about.

Instead of pushing him to tell her, she stood up to refill her apple juice and got the bottle out of the fridge. He moved over to the stove and watched as she poured the juice into a glass. "Do you want anything?"

"No, I'm good." He came up to her, hugged her tight in his arms, and pecked her forehead with a kiss. "And so are you, Marie. You're so very good. All that is good in my world."

He bent to kiss her neck in a spot that he knew tickled and she laughed as she pulled away from him. A shiver ran through her as the sensation lingered and she glared at him. "That was just wrong."

She picked up the glass to take a drink, but before she could pull it up all the way, he spoke.

"It made you smile though," he grinned at her but then the smile disappeared.

The glass shook in her hand. Her left

hand. The hand that didn't have a tremor. The juice splashed out of the glass until she put it down. There. That.

That was what really scared her, that was the elephant in the room they'd danced around all this time today. Would she need a doctor? Would she be able to travel? She looked at him, fear in her eyes, reflected back in his.

"That's the wrong hand." His voice was low as if he didn't want to say it too loud.

"I know." She stared at him, then looked at her hand, flat against the counter. "It's the wrong hand."

"Fuck." He took her in his arms again and she let the sob out that she'd been trying to strangle down. "Fuck baby, I'm here for you. Don't cry, please don't cry."

"I can't do it, Matteo, I can't go through that. Not what Mom went through. I just can't." She clung to him, her lifeline in this storm. "Please, make it go away."

"I would if I could, baby, you know that."

There were tears in his voice, but she

was clinging tightly to him, her head pressed into his neck, and she couldn't see his face. The world, the real world, had just settled back over them, and it had destroyed all of the happiness she'd had all day. It was the wrong hand.

# 17

Dinner was over with and the dishes washed. Anton had gone back upstairs, his face troubled, but he hadn't said much. They'd talked while Marie cooked dinner, and they'd both agreed it was time to go back to New York. Anton would call in the morning and arrange a plane for later tomorrow night; he hadn't told her yet. He wanted to make sure she was calm, that she wasn't a mess because that tremor in her other hand had all but wrecked them both.

She'd put a smile on her face after she'd cried herself out and he'd taken her into the living room. She'd put her head in his lap and fallen asleep. It had been one of the sweetest moments of his life, stroking her hair as she slept peacefully, at last. He hadn't wanted to move and wake her, so he watched some sappy romantic comedy that came on the television, with the closed captioning on to keep quiet. It was a trick he'd learned from her. One of the many things he'd learned from her.

He loved her, he loved her more than anything else on this planet, and nothing would ever change that. He just wished he could tell her. He'd almost told her a dozen times, maybe a thousand times, but something always held it back. It sounded like Celeste's voice, that something, telling him not to be so fucking weak. Only the poor were weak, according to her.

From what he'd seen, it was the poor that were the toughest of all; those that were rich had it easy. He'd been the spoiled nephew of a mafia queen his entire life, but that didn't mean he'd been protected from the worst things people could do to each other. He'd watched as men were beaten for information, he'd seen the things his aunt had ordered, so much worse than anything he'd ever ordered. Although, he'd done his fair share of dirty deeds, things he'd never tell Marie about.

Things he tried not to think about.

"What are you thinking about?" The sweet sound of her soft voice broke into his thoughts and he turned his head towards her.

They'd made a pallet on the floor, in front of the fire, with pillows for their heads, and a bottle of wine to ease their thirst.

He squinted into the orange flames for a moment, the heat cast off by the burning wood a nice warmth that wasn't too hot. He rolled over, tucked his left arm behind his head, and stared up at the bare beams of the ceiling. "You."

"Me? But you were frowning." She sat

up and looked down at him. "What have I done?"

"You haven't done anything." He looked up at her brown eyes, a shade he'd come to love, and smile. "Not yet anyway."

He sat up and pulled her down to tickle her ribs. She laughed loudly and tried to get away, but he held her down with a kiss that soon turned her quiet, except for a gasp here and there. Then she moaned and that sound went straight through him. "Fuck, I can't believe how much I need you, Marie."

"Crazy isn't it? Aren't we supposed to be sick of each other by now, and getting on with life?" She smiled up at him, now on her back.

"It is. I never thought I'd have anything like this. I never dared dream I would find someone to, ahem, someone like you. I didn't know you were down there in the bayou waiting on me, though."

"I was, even if I didn't know it. But my momma did tell me to stay away from Mafia boys, that you were all the same." She pushed a lock of hair behind his ear and sighed happily. "I'm so glad I ignored her."

"Are you? Even with my crazy aunt?" He hadn't necessarily meant to bring the woman up again, but he did wonder.

"Even with your crazy aunt." She looped her arms behind his head and pushed her chin up a little. "Maybe even because of your crazy aunt. She made you who you are, but despite all of that, you're still your own man. Aunt or not."

"What do you mean?" A peck on the nose accompanied the question.

"You are a strong, independent, fiercely loyal man, Matteo. You're a good man. You've lived your life, and you've come to a point where you know what you want from the rest of your life. Instead of throwing that away, you're choosing to live for yourself now. Not anyone else. Except for me, maybe." The brightness of her smile made her eyes shine and he couldn't help but love her a little more.

He pulled the blankets back up over

them and pulled her close to his chest. He needed to deflect from the emotions her confidence in him caused. He wasn't a good man, he hadn't been, at least, not until her. "I'm glad you think so highly of me."

"Why wouldn't I?" She pecked his nose this time and smiled. "You're perfect for me."

"And you are all that matters. The only person's opinion that matters is yours." He brushed the hair away from her face, looked down at her, so beautiful and full of something he wanted to say was love.

Could it be that she did? Or did she just think she was in love? He wondered sometimes. He was her first kiss, her first lover, her first in so many things. At first, that had fascinated him, but now he wondered if she'd ever wonder what life, sex, kissing even, would be like with someone else? Maybe it was unfair.

Fuck it.

He didn't care if it was fair, not when she looked up at him like that, with desire mixed with happiness. She loved him and that was all that mattered. Fucking someone else was the furthest thing from her mind, and as long as he kept her happy, didn't act like a dick and fuck this all up, he'd keep her that way.

Marie wasn't the kind of woman you could push away forever, he knew that she wasn't the kind that would be able to handle a man that was constantly a jerk to her either. She wanted a man to be a man, and act like one. To be responsible, to help her, and be her mate. Not a man that walked all over her, she'd had enough of that shit to last her a lifetime.

"Want to watch a movie?" he asked though he knew she didn't. "Or we could go to bed?"

He wiggled his eyebrows suggestively, but comically, and she laughed as he'd wanted her to. Good, he hadn't pushed too far or said too much that might scare her away. She hadn't realized it, he didn't think, but she was a caged bird waiting to be freed. She wanted to explore the world, to see how far she could go outside of that cage she'd lived in all her life.

He wanted to fly with her, that's all he asked, to be allowed to accompany her on her new journey through life.

"Sure, we can watch a movie," she said smugly as if to thwart his plans. "Maybe something like *National Lampoon's Christmas Vacation*. That always makes me laugh."

"What's it about?" He sat up and reached for the remote on the coffee table.

"You've never seen it?" Her jaw dropped and she stared at him with wide eyes.

"No, what is it? Obviously, a Christmas movie, but what's it about?"

"Oh, we have to watch it now." She took the remote from him and found the movie on one of the sites they ordered movies from. "Okay, get ready. You're going to laugh your ass off."

"We'll see." He pulled her to him, both on their sides now, and kissed her ear. "But I will be taking you to bed after."

"Yeah, yeah, hush," she laughed playfully and settled her head down on her pillow.

He saw some of the movie, but most of the time, he was watching her. She laughed through the entire thing, in a way that was so free and easy. Her eyes shone brightly, and everything about her was just… happy.

When the movie finished, he grabbed another bottle of wine and took her upstairs. While she changed, he put on some music, lit a few candles, and slid into the covers totally naked. She came back into the room with her fuzzy pink pajamas on. He frowned when she slid into the bed, but let it go. Pajamas were easy enough to take off.

"I'm so glad to be here with you." She took a deep breath, one that wasn't very steady. He knew she had a really hard time getting to sleep, and when she did, she didn't sleep for long most nights.

It was one of the things that worried him. She'd go downstairs to keep from bothering him, but he worried that she wasn't sleeping. He knew, every morning when he woke up alone, that she hadn't slept well again. She needed solid sleep, being tired all the time would just stress her out and cause more problems for her.

"Did you take a sleeping pill?" he asked, but he knew they'd been in the drawer in the nightstand since they'd come here.

"No, they don't work well, not anymore." She put her head down on his chest and wrapped herself around him. "Honestly, those stories or reading are the only things that work to help me get to sleep now. They don't help me stay asleep though. I could fall asleep right now, but I'd be awake again by two or three am."

She blew out air in frustration and he patted her shoulder. "Well, let's talk about something else. Maybe worrying about it, trying too hard, doesn't help."

"You're going to talk me to sleep, are you?" She laughed and put her hand lower on his stomach.

His senses went on alert, her hand was

almost on his hip, and he knew it made him a dog when she was so miserable about sleeping, but all he could think about was willing her hand to go lower. While she seemed to think she took a lot from him, he took just as much. He'd never wanted a woman as he did her, it was twenty-four hours a day, seven days a week, his need for her.

As she'd said earlier, he thought it would calm down after a while, but every moment he spent with her told him that he was out of luck. He'd want her like this for the rest of his life. She knew exactly how to touch him now, what made him weak with need, but more than that, her responses to him drove him wild.

"I'm going to *something* you to sleep." He tipped her face up for a kiss and groaned when her hand moved down, lower, until she grasped him in her hand.

"I guess I know what that something is," she said against his lips, a smile on her face. "Something that might just tire us both out."

"It might." He let her have her way with him and relaxed as her hand began to stroke along his length, slowly, a tease more than anything.

One last night in this bed, he thought, with her wrapped around him. He had one good thing to say about the cold out here, it meant they spent a lot of time cuddled up together for warmth. Anton would come down later and fill the stoves up to keep the fires going, but when it was in the negative digits outside, you could light as many fires as you wanted to, it was hard to stay warm.

She moved down the bed and all of his thoughts disappeared. Her lips wrapped around his tip and sucked him deeper into the wet heat of her mouth, and he forgot what words were, what he'd been thinking about, altogether. All that existed was Marie's sexy mouth and her hands.

He realized he'd moved his hands only when his fingers met her silky hair, wrapped in it to help guide the pace she used on him. When she pulled back up with heavy suction, to the very edge of his cock, his toes curled and his hips thrust up into her face.

"You're so good to me, Marie. Don't stop, baby." He didn't even know he wanted to speak, but the flow of words didn't stop. "Fuck, you suck me so good now."

The movement of her head didn't stop, but her hands moved. One cupped his balls gently, stroked them as she let him slide deeper into her throat, while her other hand reached up to gently twist one of his nipples. A low grunt pulled up from somewhere deep in his throat, and he nearly lost control.

He wanted this pleasure to last, he wanted to fuck her, but she was determined that she was going to make him come.

"Baby, you have to stop if you want me to fuck you," he strangled out. He didn't want her to stop but he wanted to fuck her too. She made the decision for him and pinched at his nipple a little bit harder just as she sucked up his length one more time.

She was totally in control and knew exactly what she wanted, so he let himself go to enjoy what she was doing.

"Have it your way," he chuckled throatily as he relaxed into the bed once again.

"Mm," was all he heard from her. That was fine, it meant her lips were still wrapped around his dick.

He opened his eyes, saw her bent over him in those terrible fuzzy pajamas, and wanted to see her naked, but let it go. Her mouth and her face were what he needed to see. He pushed her hair out of her face, held it back, and she looked directly into his eyes. Her lips were wrapped around him so prettily, and he couldn't get enough of that vision.

"That's it, Marie, suck my cock. Fuck, you do that so well." He thrust into her face eagerly, out of control now, but he kept his eyes open, glued to hers, as the first pulsing explosion shook him. He kept his eyes open as she swallowed every drop he had to give her. Her eyes were hungry, excited, then pleased as pleasure rocked him, until he couldn't hold his eyes open anymore.

He let her head go and sank into the pillows. She crawled off him to her own side of the bed to have a swallow of apple juice. After that, she cuddled up to him, perfectly content to hold him. He couldn't move, not yet. He'd just rest his eyes a little bit. She'd nearly killed him with that one, those eyes of her daring him to come in her mouth. Fuck, that was so hot.

Tomorrow, he thought as sleep took, he'd tell her tomorrow that they were leaving.

# 18

When Matteo began to snore softly, Marie rolled over and tried to keep her mind blank. She tried counting, then tried to think of nothing, but that took too much thought, and when she got tired, her mind drifted. Places she wanted to add to their list of places to go popped into her head, then she thought about things like how they'd be so happy traveling around together.

When she remembered she needed to see the doctor, she finally gave up and got out of bed. Gently, she got out of the bed and walked downstairs, her socks padding the sound of her steps. She went to the window to see the night was lit up by a full moon. Moonbeams reflected from the snow to light up the night brightly, almost enough to see the trees in the distance. Some movement caught her eyes, and she stared at it for a long time, but the movement didn't come again.

She looked around the rest of the yard that she could see and decided the raccoon must be back. Little scamp. She moved away from the window, settled down on the couch, and picked up the remote. It wasn't so late that she couldn't watch another movie. She'd just put a movie on when the power went out.

The snow had stopped the day before, there was no wind, but maybe a tree had fallen on a line somewhere out there. Or a car accident further down the mountain. She waited for the generator to come on, it was supposed to all be automatic, but nothing happened.

The sound of steps drew her to Anton as he came down the stairs. "What's going on?"

"I don't know, the generator should be on by now." He slid into a coat and put gloves on his hands. With a flick of his wrists, the hood of his coat came up over his head and he tied the strings at his throat. Stay in here, I won't be long."

Marie nodded, not sure it was a good idea for Anton to go outside on his own. The more she thought about it, the more she worried. There'd been movement outside, a movement that was too big to just be a raccoon, even if she'd told herself that's all it was.

Maybe she should go wake Matteo up. He should go out there with Anton, to keep an eye out. Marie bit at her lip, then started to click her fingernail against her teeth as worry consumed her. Anton had been out there far too long. Yeah, he had on enough clothes to stay warm, but it shouldn't take long to fix the generator. She'd started to rise, to go wake up Matteo when Anton came back in.

"I don't know what's wrong with the stupid thing, it won't start." He shivered as he took off his coat and gloves, then walked to the fire in the living room. "I'll go back out in a few minutes, I just needed to warm up."

"Just leave it until the morning." She tried to get him to change his mind. "It's too cold to be out there messing around in the dark."

"Are you kidding? It's nearly daylight out there with the full moon, I can see everything fine. I just can't get it to come on for some reason."

"Please, Anton? Just stay in here, okay? I've got this creepy feeling that I can't shake." She'd had it a few times in the night the last couple of days. Like someone was watching from the woods, only she hadn't wanted to admit it. Tonight, though, she felt like there was something evil nearby, something so bad she could actually feel it.

In Louisiana, they'd call it her gut, and tell her to listen to it. They weren't necessarily believers in the supernatural, but people in her town knew how to survive, and gut was one thing you followed. Her gut was telling her there was something bad out there and if he went back out it would get him.

"It will only…" his words faltered as she gave him a pleading look. "Alright, fine, but if Matteo gets mad you better tell him it was your idea."

"I will, I promise." She reached up quickly, pecked his cheek, and then stepped away, her cheeks red. "Sorry, didn't mean to invade your space."

He ducked his head, but she saw the grin on his face. "It's okay. I'll go back up then, keep an eye out."

"Alright, I think I'll try going back to bed. Maybe without the hum of electricity in this place, I can get to sleep."

When she crawled into the bed Matteo

turned to her, still half asleep. "What's wrong?"

"The power went out and Anton can't get the generator to start. I told him to leave it until the morning. It will probably need two pairs of hands and a lot of light to find the problem."

"Okay," he said and promptly started to snore again.

A pleased smile crept across her face as she held him to her. The house was really quiet, and she felt safer here with him. Maybe she'd overreacted, she thought as she began to relax, and sleep came to take her. It was probably just an animal outside, nothing more than that. She'd see in the morning, when the light was bright and warm, that there'd been nothing to be afraid of.

LARGE POOLS of water stood between her and Matteo, and her feet were already cold.

How was she going to get across all of that water to get to him? He beckoned to her from the other side, so far away, and she wanted to run to him, but the water was in the way. She moaned in helplessness just as she smelled smoke.

When she turned around, she saw a wall of fire behind her, ready to consume her if she didn't run into the water. A lick of flame reached out for her, turned into the shape of a human hand as the first tendrils of heat burned wisps of her hair and warmed her cheek, she started to scream, turned, and tripped as the flame came even closer. Another scream woke her up and she opened her eyes as she realized it was only a dream.

Her heart still thudded in her chest and it took her a moment to calm down. The dream had felt so real, she could still smell the smoke. She took one final breath and tried to close her eyes, but she frowned. That smoke wasn't just from the dream.

Was Anton refilling the stoves? No, this was too strong.

"Matteo, wake up, I think something is wrong." She shook him just as Anton came racing down the stairs to bang on their door.

"Fire, wake up everybody, the house is on fire!" Matteo woke up and grabbed a robe and some shoes, while Marie did the same.

"What the fuck is happening?" Matteo demanded, still half asleep but functioning.

"I don't know. I woke up, smelled the smoke, and thought it was my nightmare, or Anton filling the stoves. I decided to wake you and then he came down. Hurry, grab your phone and wallet. Let's get out."

"Fuck, where are the keys?" He looked around on his nightstand, found them, and put them in his pocket. He grabbed the clothes they'd had on yesterday, and then ushered her out of the door.

She had her bag in her hands and her phone was already in the pocket of her robe. She'd scooped her medicines into her bag in one fell swoop, slipped on her snow-boots, and was ready. The smoke was getting thicker the longer they were inside, and Anton was all but breaking the door down banging on it. "Let's get out of here."

"Wait, I forgot something." He went to a dresser drawer, pulled out a pistol, and put that in his other pocket. "Let's go."

Marie stayed quiet about the weapon, she didn't care right now, she just wanted out of the house. They came down the stairs in a rush, the sound of the fire a raging roar that scared her shitless. She looked around as they came down the stairs and saw that the fire was at the front door too.

"We can't get out there," she cried and turned back to Matteo with a mask of fear on her face.

"We can do this, Marie, just stay calm. Here, put this over your face." She'd started to cough as he spoke.

The sweater he had on yesterday helped

to mask some of the fumes, but it was hard to breathe.

"Okay, jump over the banister and head to the kitchen. We'll go out the window in there." Tears from the smoke filled his eyes as he spoke close to her ear. "We will be right behind you. You can do this, Marie."

"I can, I can." She nodded but then she looked back at the front door. The flames had started to climb to the ceiling and the entire living room was already hidden by nothing but orange and blue flames. Acrid smoke filled the air, filled her lungs, and made her hair stink.

One more deep breath, a final look at Matteo, and then she went over the banister. She dropped down, stayed low, and headed into the kitchen. She couldn't hear anything now but the roar of the fire as it ate away at the walls, the furniture, everything in the beautiful cabin she'd felt so safe in for so long now.

"You can do it! Keep going, Marie!" She

heard Matteo shout over the roar of the fire.

She kept going, almost crawling, but she reached the windows in the kitchen. The flames weren't in here yet, but the room was full of smoke. She waited for Matteo and Anton but opened the window to breathe fresh air. It was cold air, but she didn't care, the heat in the house was unbelievable now, and she wanted to go out, wanted to run for the SUV, but couldn't leave, not until Matteo caught up to her.

She was about to go back and look for him when he and Anton came into the room together. She hugged him quickly as Anton went out of the window first, followed by Matteo, then Marie. Matteo caught her and they headed for the warmth the SUV would offer them as they looked back at the house, the back side, the side where all the bedrooms were, was completely in flames. Marie stopped and gasped as she saw the flames climb onto the roof and begin to move swiftly.

"Come on, Marie. Get in the car, honey," Matteo urged, just as a shot rang out from the trees in the distance. "Fuck."

"Get down!" he called and all three of them dropped. He hit the button on the SUV, which gave away where they were headed, but it didn't matter, it was their only way off this mountain.

"Stay down but move fast. We can do this Marie, we can. Don't get up until we're at the car, okay?" His face was easy to see in the moonlight, and the assurance in his eyes helped her to ignore the cold, wet snow that was soaking into her pajamas and left her shivering. She hadn't even put a coat on before they left the house, just her robe.

"Yes, I understand." There was terror in her voice and her face but she didn't care. She was too terrified to try to hide it. "We can do this."

"We can, baby, with each other. Come on now, let's move. It's going to be dangerous, baby, but it's our only way out."

Another shot rang out of the darkness,

but they made it to the car before any more shots were fired.

Matteo stood up with Marie and she damned the idiot that thought turning lights on in cars when you opened the door was a good idea. It wasn't now. It gave them away completely. Anton went around the other side, climbed in, and closed the door. Matteo was just about to shut the door on Marie's side when another burst of shots rang out, over and over again, until she thought it would go on forever. "Matteo!"

She screamed his name, but he only closed the door as he grunted and pulled away. She saw him fall in the snow, but he got up and crawled to the other side of the car. Anton was on a burner phone, calling the fire department and reporting shots fired as well.

Matteo climbed into the car, pain creasing his face.

"What's wrong? Did they get you?" Marie's voice quavered, but he just shut the door and took a deep breath. "Matteo?"

He put his hands calmly on the steering wheel, put the keys in the ignition, and started the SUV as more shots pinged off the body of the car. "We have to get out of here."

"Matteo, are you shot?" she demanded to know as he gritted his teeth, hit the switch on the gate, and put the car into gear.

"It's just a graze, baby, nothing more. Put your seatbelt on." He pushed down the accelerator and they were off just as the sounds of the police and fire trucks started to come up the mountain faintly. Matteo looked behind him at the red and white glow of the lightbars on the trucks as he sped by them a few minutes later, but he didn't see a vehicle following their car.

"I think whoever it was must be on foot, there's no car following us." He grunted with pain before he went on. "They must have walked up. "Fuck, what the hell happened?"

He turned to look back at Anton before he switched his gaze back to the road.

"The power went off earlier and I couldn't get the generator running. It's been so quiet..." Anton stated, but Marie interrupted.

"I told him to leave it until the morning. I had a feeling it wasn't going to start, and we had the fires. I never thought about it killing the floodlights or the security cameras. It's my fault."

"No, the one to blame is the one that paid for this shit. That's who's at fault, not you two." Matteo drove down the mountain carefully, aware that they could still be in danger, but needing to be safe.

She'd seen a few spots of black ice on the road and knew his mission now, as always, was to keep her safe. She felt terrible that he was in danger because of her.

"How is your leg?" she asked because she couldn't see the leg that had been shot. It was his left leg and out of her line of sight.

"It's okay, but it burns. Just a graze, babe,

don't worry." He patted her hand then put his hand back on the steering wheel.

"Where are we going? Shouldn't we talk to the fire department, the cops?" Marie asked, but Matteo didn't look at her.

"We don't call the cops in our world, Marie. We just don't." He gripped the steering wheel harder and drove onto the main highway that bypassed the town and headed north.

"Okay, I accept that. But where are we going?" She was nervous, scared, and she saw that he understood that. They were all tired, they'd just been woken up in the middle of the night with the house on fire and someone had shot at them.

"I didn't see any of them, did you, Anton? All I heard was shots, then my leg was on fire. They hit me, which means whoever has paid for the contract doesn't care who is killed, as long as Marie is taken out. Fucking hell."

She felt even worse now, she thought, and let her head fall down to the window.

That was when she noticed they were still in their nightclothes.

"Do you two have your passports with you?" he asked. She knew they did, it had been something he and Anton had discussed before they left New York and he'd made sure she brought hers with her. He must want to be sure Anton had his.

"Yes," Anton and Marie replied, but neither sounded enthusiastic right now.

He saw a rest stop and pulled in there to change into the clothes they'd dropped last night into the hamper in their bedroom. She wasn't happy about changing in the car, but it was better than going into a cold, empty, too brightly lit public bathroom at this hour. She hurriedly changed while Anton inspected the car where it had taken shots.

Matteo called him back in when they were dressed in jeans and sweatshirts again. He'd wrapped a length of bandage from a first aid kit Marie found in the glove box around his leg. It wasn't much, a graze, but it was still bleeding a little. Hopefully, it would stop soon, she thought as Anton got back into the car.

"Right then, we're going to Canada," he said as he stared out of the window, the orange glow of morning already brightening the horizon. "Everything alright with the car, Anton?"

"Looks like a bit of body damage but I don't see anything that will cause a problem. It's mainly in the back end on the hatch." Anton, who'd been dressed all night and hadn't needed to change shut his door and settled into his seat. "I think the car will be fine. We should make it to Canada, no problem."

Marie was nervous; too nervous to sleep, too nervous to stay awake. Matteo saw her struggling and pulled off at an all-night gas station. He filled up the SUV, while she and Anton got them all coffee and some snacks, then they were back on the road.

Anton's phone rang a half-hour later

and he answered. They could hear him talking but not what the caller said.

"That was the police. They wanted to know why we left. I told them someone had set the house on fire and when we went outside, shots were fired at us. They still want to talk to us." He knew they'd heard his side but repeated it all so it made sense this time.

"Fuck that, we're going to Canada. Pay the owner whatever he wants and send him my apologies. I didn't mean to get their cabin burned down." Marie could hear the guilt in Matteo's voice, but it wasn't his fault either. She put her hand on his thigh and squeezed to let him know he wasn't alone.

"Will do, boss."

"Thanks. Then, find out how the fuck they found us."

"I'm guessing they looked for me. Someone must have noticed I was gone and figured I'd left with you. I wasn't trying to hide where I was by not using my debit or credit cards, which was stupid of me. I take full responsibility."

"No, don't blame yourself, Anton," Marie started, and Matteo instantly agreed.

"We weren't sure about that, we talked about it, remember? We thought they'd take a lot longer to notice you were gone too. Damn, they're sneaky bastards." Matteo gripped the steering wheel harder, then took a sip of his coffee. "Marie, I suggest you put your headphones on, find something to listen to, and get some sleep. This will take a few hours."

"Around three, boss," Anton said from the back seat. "There's a place called Creston, in British Columbia, just across the border. Looking for hotels now."

"Great. We'll stop as soon as we get over the border then. When we get there, Marie, just answer their questions politely and smile at them. We're traveling around and wanted to head over to Vancouver for a visit. Just a trip for pleasure for a week, then we're headed back home. Anton, make reservations on my phone for somewhere in Vancouver, two rooms, use that credit card that we have in my dead uncle's name."

Marie wasn't really paying attention, but she saw him wince when he said that part about the credit card. It didn't bother her, she never knew her father - his uncle by marriage. It was a good idea, to keep a credit card in someone's name that wasn't theirs, she thought. She tried to get some sleep, but her head kept banging against the window, or her feet would get cold, even with the heat on. So she spent most of the drive staring out of the window as an audiobook played in her ears.

At one point, she heard the back window open and then close not long after. "Burner phone's gone, boss."

"Good idea. We'll figure out how to talk to them later if we have to. For now, I'd rather keep us out of it."

When they reached the border, the Canadian border patrol guy was friendly. He chatted with them, checked their pass-

ports, then let them through without a lot
of questions. Anton had mentioned the
bullet holes in the back might draw some
attention, but Marie suspected the guy just
wanted to get back into the building where
it was warm so ignored those.

They arrived in a place called Creston
just as the sun came up. It was a small
town, neat and tidy, with a huge mountain in the background. Marie watched as
the fog began rolling down the massive
thing in the distance. It was amazing and
she liked the look of the town. It wasn't a
massive city like Vancouver, but more
like her kind of place. Quiet, with enough
shops that you could find whatever you
needed, and full of people that were smiling, even at the early hour they
arrived at.

The motel they decided to stop at
wouldn't let them check in until 11 am, so
they drove around until they found a café
that served breakfast. In quiet, they ate the
meals they'd ordered, drank a few cups of

coffee, then left after paying with the same dead man's credit card.

Marie's back hurt, her legs felt like they were frozen solid, and her eyes felt like they were full of sand. She looked over at Matteo and wanted to cry.

"By the time we get some supplies, fill up the car, and get back to the motel, we can check in to our rooms."

She smiled gratefully and walked with the men when they stopped at a grocery store. She found some antibiotic ointment and more bandages for his leg, and some pain relievers in case he got a fever. And for the headache that made it feel as if her eyes were pulsing with her every heartbeat.

"I feel like we haven't slept in days," Marie said when they were finally allowed into the room. It wasn't anything near like she knew Matteo was used to, it was a cheap motel, but it was clean and tidy. She went directly to the bed and slid in between the covers. She didn't care if Matteo had paid for the most expensive room, the one with a huge hot tub, or that it was the middle of the day, she needed to sleep.

"You rest, babe. I'm going to talk to Anton," Matteo said softly, but he stopped when she sat up a little.

"You need to sleep, you both do. We're safe for now, come get some rest." She held the covers up - a white sheet, a fuzzy pink blanket, and a tacky pink and blue floral bedspread - to invite him in.

"I will in a bit, I just need to talk to him. It's fine, really." He kissed her forehead then left the room.

She'd cleaned up his leg again at a gas station before they crossed the border. She'd put a new bandage on it, but she still thought he needed to stay off of it and rest. He wouldn't listen, though. She was too tired to fight him, she decided, and pulled the covers up over her head. She'd change the bandage later, add the antibiotic ointment, and make sure he rested. After she had a little nap, just a little one. That's all.

Hours later, when the sun had set and

the room was dark, she heard Matteo and Anton talking. She hadn't wanted to sleep so long, she'd be awake all night now, but she felt rested at least. When she realized what they were talking about she went still and tried to even out her breath.

"I think it's Celeste, which is why we're using that card. She doesn't know about it because she doesn't bother the accountant. As long as the money's coming in, she doesn't care about anything else. It's been open since the day he died."

"Strange how they didn't cut that one off, after he died, I mean," Anton mused. They were at a tiny table in the corner with cups of coffee, away from the tiny dresser with the flatscreen TV sitting on top of it. The hot tub was in the space where the other double bed would normally be.

Marie thought it was a little tacky to have the tub in the room with them but wouldn't turn down a chance to get in it. Her muscles ached all over, but Matteo should stay out of it with his leg, so maybe she'd just have a shower instead.

"She didn't bother to send in the paperwork and the accountant didn't either. We'll use that one until we figure out if it's safe to go back to New York yet."

"Alright, boss. I'll go pick us up some food and come back in a little while."

"Yeah, she'll probably be hungry. Bring plenty of water back too, she'll be thirsty."

"Will do."

He left and Matteo came to the other side of the bed and slipped in. "You awake, Marie?"

His New York accent wasn't as pronounced when he was in public, but sometimes, when he was with her, it came back. She found it endearing and turned to hug him with a grin. "I am. I'm alive, I'm fine, and as you said, thirsty."

"I thought you would be, so I got some bottles of water for you at the grocery store earlier. There's juice too if you want that. I have apples, tangerines, and some chips to snack on until Anton gets back if you want them. He's getting us all the special over at that bar and grill across the street."

"That sounds good. How's your leg?" She turned to face him properly and cuddled close.

"It's sore, but I'll live. Just a scratch really." He brushed it off, but she thought he was brave.

"It could have ended up anywhere, and all you cared about was getting me in the car. You saved me, again."

"I protected you, it's my job." He shrugged off her praise and slid his hand down her back. "I'm just glad it was me that got the graze and not you. I couldn't live with myself if you'd been hit."

"Not to mention you'd have gone crazy on the guy." She knew him enough now to know that was true.

"You are correct." He dotted a kiss on her nose before he left the bed. "Tonight's entertainment includes crappy television, a game of cards, or reading. I'd like us to keep all electronics off for a while. There's a store across the street that sells second-hand books if you want to have a look later."

"That sounds good. What about clothes?" She looked down at her jeans and wondered how long she could wear them before they started to smell grungy.

"That we've already taken care of." Matteo pointed to the closet and she went to it. She found a new pack of cotton panties in her size, a couple of bras, a pack of socks, three sweaters, four pairs of jeans, a couple of sweatshirts, and shoes - all cheap but serviceable. They'd work until they figured out their next move.

"Great." She found another bag and found her favorite kind of fleece pajamas, a couple of nightgowns, and some flannel pajamas too. "Thanks."

"I see you like your sleepwear, at least." He sat down at the table and looked at her. "I'm really sorry about this."

"Don't be Matteo, it's not your fault, it

really isn't. I think we know who is behind this, don't we? There's only one person smart enough to track Anton, only one person that would know you'd bring him with you: Celeste."

Pain crossed his face in a dark flash, but he frowned and then finally looked up, resigned. "It has to be her."

"It does." She felt terrible for him, but it was true. Celeste was the only one that could figure all of that out.

"Why don't you get a shower, wash all that smoke off you, and I'll wait for Anton, okay? I got you some shampoo, conditioner, a toothbrush and toothpaste earlier, when you were in zombie mode." He chuckled and she glared at him.

"I was exhausted after all of that. I barely even remember being at the store. It's a good thing you were awake."

"I was tired too, babe, but you've never experienced something like that."

"Have you?" she asked quickly, curious.

"Not the fire part, but the being shot at

part? A time or two. Which is part of the reason I'm wanting to get out of this game." The way lines appeared at the side of his eyes, and the tightness of his mouth was enough to tell her how thoughts of his past troubled him.

She nodded and walked into the bathroom, her new fuzzy pajamas in hand. She had a brush in her bag so she could brush her hair out later, but that wasn't what was on her mind. His aunt had put him in a life that meant he'd get shot at. What kind of woman would do that to her own nephew?

# 19

---

"I want you to go to Italy, find my aunt, and find out if she's the one behind this contract," Matteo said into the phone. He was outside of their hotel room, while Marie was in the shower, cleaning off the smoke and filth from the night before.

"Sure, Matteo. I can do that," Petey said from the other end of the line as Matteo breathed in relief. He wasn't sure how the other man would feel about the job.

"You don't have to do anything, just find out what you can. She'll have started the contract over there if she is the one behind it. Someone there will know." Matteo sighed, exhaustion was creeping in, even though he'd had a nap earlier. It had been a long day, and it still wasn't over. Not yet.

"No problem, Matteo. Anything for you, you know that. I'll get a plane out tonight. Just tell me where she is, or where you think she is, and I'll find my way there."

"Thanks, Petey." He gave the man the details that he could, which wasn't much, just the name of the town and the villa where she was staying. "If you need to, get some money from Penelope. If not, just turn in an invoice to her when you're done, whatever you need to do. I'll pay for it all."

"Got ya, boss. You be careful out there, alright?" Petey sounded concerned, which Matteo understood, this was a very dicey situation. He and Petey had worked to-gether for a long time. He'd learned to trust him, and the man worked every single day to ensure that trust stayed rock solid.

"Will do, Petey. You take care, and let me know as soon as you find out anything."

Matteo ended the call just as Marie opened the door to their room.

"You didn't get me a coat." She stood there with her hair dripping down her back, wrapped in one of the white towels provided by the motel, obviously confused.

"Fuck, I'm sorry baby." He smacked his hand against his forehead and ushered her back in, out of the cold. "We'll get you one tomorrow, I promise."

"Okay. I was about to dry off when it hit me, you didn't get me a coat."

"I didn't get me one either. Anton managed to grab more than we did, so he has a coat, but it just never entered my head. I'm really sorry." He felt completely stupid for forgetting the one thing they'd need the most right now. How could he forget that? People would notice if they continued to walk around in freezing cold Canada without coats.

Not like the gunshots or the American plates on the car would draw enough attention, he had to go and forget to get the coats, too.

"It's alright. Like you said, we'll do it tomorrow. Sit down, let me look at your leg." She tucked the towel back in between her breasts when she sat down and that distracted him while she pulled his leg up into her lap. He was completely engrossed in watching a bead of water slide down from her hair, straight into her cleavage when she ripped the bandage off of his leg.

He wasn't massively hairy, but there was hair on his leg. So it was probably best she just ripped it like that, but it didn't help to stop the scream of pain he let out. "Fuck, Marie, that hurt!"

"Sorry, but it's done now. Hand me those alcohol wipes out of the bag on the nightstand there." They were sitting on the bed so he reached over to grab the bag without having to move too much. "It doesn't look bad. But I want to keep it clean."

She probably didn't realize she did it,

but her left hand, cupped around his calf while she wiped at the edges of the wound with her right, massaged his leg lovingly as if to soothe him. It was one of the things he loved about her. She always had a need to touch him, to soothe him when he was upset, or hurt, like now. Her touch was an act of love for her.

She didn't touch just anyone, and he'd noticed she didn't like people to invade her space very often, but with him, she was different. She had to touch him, be near him if they were in the same room. She needed him in her space, and that told him a lot about how she felt towards him.

"You're very sweet, Marie," he said without thinking.

"What?" She looked up, her eyebrows raised as she looked at him. "Because I'm doing something anyone else could do?"

"No, it's how you do it, babe. It's all in how you do it."

Before she could respond, Anton knocked on the door. "It's me, guys."

"Come in," Matteo called.

Marie quickly applied more antibiotic ointment to his wound, covered it with another large self-adhesive bandage, and went into the bathroom to change. He'd forgotten she was only in a towel until he saw her blush when Anton walked in. "Sorry, babe, forgot."

"It's alright," she called over her shoulder. "I'll be right back."

"Sorry, Anton."

"For what?" The other man looked up with a question on his face.

"She wasn't dressed yet. I didn't even think about it."

"That's why I keep my head down, boss." Anton grinned and brought in two bags filled with food and drinks. "I wasn't sure how hungry anybody would be, so I got desserts too, and a few more drinks."

"That should tide us over." Matteo started to take out plastic cutlery, then the boxes of food.

Marie came back out in her new pajamas, and they all ate in silence. They were all hungry but as soon as the initial hunger was sated, they began to speak.

"We'll leave in the morning, head over to Calgary, maybe?" Matteo said and sat back in his chair to let his last bite settle in before he went on. "I think we should head for Ontario, get as close to New York as we can, maybe."

"Might be a good idea," Anton agreed, but Marie didn't.

"Why go so close? We might as well head straight back to New York if we're going to be so close to it." She didn't look convinced of the proposal.

"It was a suggestion. What do you think?" He was curious to know her thoughts. She wasn't a stupid person, after all, and he respected her opinion.

"I think we should head over to Oregon or Washington. They'll expect us to be up here, or in New York, maybe even in California, but they won't expect us in some where like that. Idaho is too close to

Montana, so I don't think that's a good idea either. Or back down, to Texas maybe, or Mexico."

"Good points, all good points." Matteo saw Anton agreed when he nodded along with Matteo.

"Shall we head to warmer locations then? That sounds good to me." He shivered as he thought about more snow. "I've about had my fill of snow for the year."

"I thought all you Yankees lived for snow," Marie teased with an impish grin. "You're all the Vikings of America, built with fortitude and ice in your veins."

"Not all of us," Matteo answered with a grin of his own. "Some of us have wanted to escape to the tropics for years now."

"I'm with you there, Matteo. I'm sick to death of snow," Anton spoke up, gave Marie a shy smile, then looked back down at the chocolate cake he'd started on after his dinner.

Matteo knew it wasn't a crush that made Anton so nervous around Marie, it was that she was his wife and he wanted to be re-spectful. Anton wasn't used to speaking with women of Marie's status, and that made him nervous, shy, and almost boyish. It had caught Matteo off-guard at first, but now he was used to it. It was good to see he was relaxing though.

"Right, so Texas then down to Mexico?" Matteo asked and the other two in the room nodded. "Good. Tomorrow?"

"Yep," Marie agreed and reached for the butterscotch pie Anton had brought. "Sounds good to me."

"Sounds good, boss."

"Good. Hand me that cheesecake, will you?" Matteo took the confection from Anton and looked around. They'd need to buy more clothes again, but that would be fine, he thought with a quiet laugh. It would be nice to be warm again, without the need for a heat source other than the sun.

They spent the rest of the evening making plans, checking the route down, and were about to head to their respective beds when Anton had a thought.

"I had all of the cameras backed up to a cloud." He'd been about to stand up to leave but settled back down. He grabbed the cheap laptop he'd bought earlier and opened it up. The motel wifi was free, so he was able to get online and check the cloud where he stored the camera feeds. "I'm going to let you two get back to sleep, but I'm going to go over these feeds. Whoever set the fire must be on the feeds some-where. He got close enough to cut the power and set a fire, there must be some-thing in the footage."

"Right, let me know in the morning what you find. Good thinking, Anton."

"Thanks, Matteo."

By the time they were settled in bed, Marie was watching a movie on TV but Matteo was falling asleep. He'd just fallen into a nice, black place when a knock came at the door.

He got up and opened it, it could only be Anton, after all. "What's up?"

He knew it had to be important because Anton would have waited until the morning to come back otherwise.

"I've found something. I forgot that cameras had their own batteries. They kept recording and backed themselves up to the cloud, even after the power went out."

"How? Wouldn't they have needed wifi?" Matteo was sleepy and confused, maybe even a little pissy, but he tried to hide it.

"They weren't cheap cameras, boss." Anton came in and opened his laptop before he turned back to Matteo and Marie. "I got cameras that operated on solar energy, so the batteries were constantly charged up. I used it on the whole system, except for the monitors, those were plugged into the house electricity. I didn't think about it last night, but the wifi, the backup system, it was all on the solar power panel I'd set up on the roof."

"I didn't know you'd done that, I'm impressed," Matteo said, some of the pissiness melting away.

"I do it on all the places you have me set up security cameras. Just in case. So, the cameras were still running, still backing up into the cloud, even after the power went out. I kept patrolling, going from window to window, but the perpetrator must have waited for me to move before they set the fire."

"You have them, I take it?" Matteo asked, impatient now that some kind of information was at hand.

"I do. And you won't believe who it is." Anton hit the play button on his laptop's screen as Matteo and Marie moved forward on the bed to have a look.

There was nothing on the screen at first that wasn't normal: the outer perimeter of the house, a bunny that had got in somehow, and then, low to the ground, a figure started to move. They crawled up to the back of the house and for a moment, the screen flickered.

"What's that?" Matteo asked, and Anton nodded.

"I changed to the other camera, I spliced this all together so it would make sense and I wouldn't have to switch between feeds."

"You're good," Matteo said absently, his eyes back on the screen.

The figure, clearly visible in the bright moonlight, stood up, and actually looked at the camera before they looked away. Anton backed the video up and hit pause.

"Fuck," Matteo said with heat in his voice. Anton was right, he couldn't believe who it was.

"What? Who is she?" Marie asked as she stared at the face. It was mostly covered with a hood and a strip of cloth that went over the mouth and nose, but the eyes were clear to see. "Matteo, say something!"

"It's my cousin, Fiona. She's a bit... on the fringe of the family. I haven't seen her in years. I'd heard she'd become an assassin, but I didn't believe it." He ran his fingers through his hair and stared at Anton glacially. "I think we know what this means."

"Celeste." Anton agreed with a nod of his head.

"Has to be. If Petey can get more proof, I'll nail her ass to a wall and leave her there to rot." Matteo stood up, too angry to stay still. His own cousin had set fire to the place where he was living? Had shot him? Fuck, what the hell was wrong with his family?

"She's your cousin?" Marie asked softly, her face wreathed in disbelief. "I know my family is shitty as hell, but that's your cousin?"

"I know, hard to believe isn't it?" He sat back down, took her hand, and looked at her intently. "I'll keep you safe from her, I promise. Somehow, I'll do it. If I have to die to protect you, I will."

"Please don't say that," Marie answered in a rush, her eyes full of tears. "Don't tell me you'll die to protect me, I couldn't stand it."

"It's the truth, baby. Always."

"Still, try not to, alright?" She leaned over to kiss his cheek and then looked at Anton. "That goes for you too, buddy. Don't die for me. I couldn't take it if that happened. I just couldn't."

"Nobody's going to die, okay? I'll make sure of it." Anton said, his voice tight as he looked away from her tears.

Matteo had no idea how either of them would keep their promises, but he knew one thing, he meant to keep his. Even if she didn't want him to.

# 20

A year had passed since she first set eyes on Matteo. A year since her mother died. A year since they'd married. A year since she'd first noticed a tremor in her right hand. A few months since she was first attacked. A few weeks since their first anniversary. A few days since she'd noticed a tremor in her left hand. A few days since the fire. A few days since they were shot at and Matteo was grazed with a bullet.

A few days since she'd crossed her first international border, she thought as they pulled up to the border patrol on the American side this time. Matteo handed over their passports and the guard, one of those military-looking guys with hard eyes and thin lips, checked each passport carefully, did something with them, asked them a few questions, and then waved them on.

When Matteo handed the passports over to Marie to put back in the glovebox she was a little disappointed to see there was no stamp. She didn't understand the ins and outs of border control, but she thought there'd be stamps when she went in and left a country. She still had an empty passport, free of foreign ink. Oh well, she thought, she'd been at least. Even if her passport didn't say so.

He drove on, his gaze on the road. The sun glanced off the windshield and made it a little hard to see so he put the visor down. It was still early morning and their plans had changed a little. They were going to a small airfield in Idaho where Anton had arranged for them to meet a private plane. They'd take the plane down to Brownsville, Texas, stay the night there, then pick up an RV that Anton had rented with another credit card that Matteo gave to him. They'd leave as soon as they picked the vehicle up the next morning, headed for Mexico so it didn't matter if anyone picked up that they were in an RV in Texas.

They'd talked about this, driving around like gypsies in an RV or a tour bus, living on the road, free and wild. But they were being hunted, by a woman that was a trained assassin it would seem. Marie wondered if Celeste had anything to do with the woman's training, had she orchestrated that woman's life as she had Matteo's?

She drew a frowning face in the condensation of her window and then swiped it away. The honeymoon phase wasn't over, it had just taken a turn for the... adventurous, that was the right word, she decided.

"Uh, boss, it seems we're wanted for

questioning," Anton piped up from the backseat. "I'm taking care of it though."

"What the fuck are you talking about now?" Matteo snapped, but when Marie's head snapped around to glare at him for being mean to the other man, she saw his eyes close as he took a deep breath. He glanced at her, a look of apology on his face. "Sorry, Anton, what's up?"

"The authorities want to question us about the fire at the cabin. I got an email from the owner. He's happy with his compensation but says the police want to talk to us. I've sent them the footage of Fiona setting the fire, and shooting at us. It's harder to see her when she's shooting, but she came up close enough to continue firing that the camera caught it before the fire destroyed the equipment in the attic. That should settle that."

"Good. I did not want to go back to Montana, not for that." He relaxed a little and she put her hand on his leg. He had so much on his shoulders right now. "I'm okay, babe. We'll be at the airfield in another ten minutes or so, okay?"

"Alright. Can we stop and get something to eat first? I'm hungry." They'd left the motel without eating, they'd just packed up their stuff, checked out, and left. Her stomach was a twisting growling knot in her abdomen now.

"Sure, my love. Anton, you want anything?" he asked as he pulled up to the first fast-food place they came across. He ordered them all meals with coffee and she sorted his coffee out and unwrapped his sausage biscuit for him to eat while he drove. She ate her biscuits, with an obscene amount of sausage gravy slathered over it, quickly.

It was food, and she needed food, she said to herself as she ate the unhealthy meal. Normally, she tried to stay on the healthy side, but she made exceptions. It was comfort food for her more than anything, and when she was done, she put all of her guilty feelings away. Her stomach was happy now and that was what mattered.

Matteo followed Anton's directions to the airfield and she saw a shiny jet sitting beside a hangar, ready to go. They quickly parked the car, which would be retrieved at a later date by the owner, with repair costs already put on yet another credit card, and they boarded the plane.

The pilot was already in place and they took their seats as someone closed the door and locked it in place.

"We're ready when you are," Anton said to the pilot who gave him a thumbs up.

The mid-size jet was made for long-haul flights and would make the flight with plenty of fuel left, Matteo had told her earlier. As the pilot started the take-off procedure she looked around. It was a narrow plane, but the plush leather seats were luxurious and she had plenty of room to stretch out.

A dark-haired woman with a kind smile came around and made sure they were ready before she went to sit down herself and buckle in. Another plane trip, another moment of fleeing. Was it all worth it? Matteo had spent a small fortune on this flight alone, what had he paid for damages to the car and the cabin? What did he pay for the equipment, the clothes, Anton's time?

For a moment, she thought about fleeing, running from them both. She had a bit of money in her purse, money she'd collected here and there when Matteo gave her cash to buy things with. It would keep her for a few months if she was careful. And maybe she could find a job somewhere that wouldn't ask too many questions.

She'd file for divorce and he would be able to get on with his life. He'd said he'd be happy to give up his life in New York, and so far he'd proven that he was honest about that, but later, would he regret giving up all of that for some woman that probably couldn't even get a job as a waitress?

She tapped her thumbnail against her

teeth and stared out of the window as they launched into the air finally, but she didn't see any of it, she was too caught up in her thoughts to see it. She could wait until they were both asleep tonight, ask the hotel manager to call her a taxi to the bus station, and catch a bus back to Louisiana, maybe.

He wouldn't look for her there, and neither would Fiona the assassin. He wouldn't think she'd go back there and Fiona would assume she was with Matteo. She'd be safe for a while anyway, and so would he.

Her eyes cut to him in the seat to her left and she saw he was staring out of his own window. After the aircraft leveled out, he let his head fall back and he closed his eyes. Within moments his chest settled into an even rhythm. He was that fucking tired, she told herself. That's because of you, you stupid twit.

But, as she watched him sleep, the pain that came every time she thought of being without him overwhelmed her senses. Tears sprang to her eyes and she couldn't breathe. She couldn't leave him, it would hurt too much. God, she'd thought about it so many times, for his own good, but every single time, panic took hold and she had to stop the thoughts or she'd suffocate.

She unbuckled the seatbelt and pushed the seat back to relax with her feet up. The woman with dark hair came back and offered her a drink. Marie asked for ginger ale and hoped it would calm her stomach. Anton was in the seat in front of Matteo, on guard even though the plane was in the air.

She calmed her thoughts and opened a book on the new tablet Matteo bought for her. She was reading books in the public domain since she didn't have to register for an account to read those, and opened a tale of mystery and woe from 1920. It was amazing to read the thoughts the writer had expressed about how life would be now that the Great War had ended, how full of hope the author was about the future. A future that would see war breaking out barely

20 years later in Europe - the start of World War II.

Depression settled over her for a moment as she thought about history, the current state of the world, and her place in it. All she'd wanted was to not lose her home and maybe have a chance with a man that she'd loved even before she really knew him. She'd sensed that he was the man for her, even back then, and it was more than just sex and nothing at all to do with the money. The money only made their escape easier.

She loved him. She loved the boy that he'd been, and the man he'd hidden away under the veneer his depraved aunt had polished over him with layer after layer of cruelty. His happiness was all she wanted, and he'd told her more than once that she made him happy.

The woman came back and offered Marie a blanket. Marie took it, covered herself, and continued with the book. She'd only been reading for 20 minutes when her eyes closed and she fell asleep. She didn't know she was that tired still, but it was obvious when she woke up that she'd been asleep for a while. She hadn't changed position and her hip ached on that side. She went to the bathroom, glanced at Matteo, and saw he was still asleep.

The woman came back, offered her a rather fancy looking sandwich and Marie took it gratefully. Turkey on ham, with lettuce and tomatoes, with a pack of mustard spread over it, was just what she needed. She opened her book back up, sipped at another can of ginger ale, and ate her sandwich.

Before long, the pilot let them know they'd be landing and the woman came back to wake up Anton and Matteo both. The men stretched, buckled in, and before they knew it, they were on the ground in Houston. Marie put her coat over her arm, grabbed her bag, and walked off the plane with a wave to the woman.

"Well, here we are. It's 2:15 pm, 72 degrees, and the sky is clear. What do you guys want to do?" Anton asked them, and they both looked at each other.

"Let's get to the hotel and relax for a bit. We have a long drive tomorrow and we'll want to be rested for that."

"As you wish." Anton smiled and went to ask about getting a taxi. One arrived ten minutes later and they packed their meager belongings into the car, all in new suitcases, and Anton told the driver where they wanted to go. Houston was huge, amazing, and so warm compared to Montana and British Columbia. Marie was getting hot underneath the black sweater she had on and wanted her t-shirt and shorts back, with a pair of flip flops to go with it.

"I want to go shopping, Matteo. If I take Anton with me, do you think it would be alright?" she asked as the taxi pulled up to the hotel they'd reserved. He was in the front seat and turned to look at her with concern.

"I'd rather be with you, but, uh, yeah. I

guess. I'll get us checked in and text Anton
with our room numbers. Here, use this
card." He reached in his wallet and took out
one of quite a few cards he kept in there.
She knew it would be another secret account he had but didn't ask about it.

"I won't stay out long. I'm just going to
get us a few things more suitable for the
weather."

"There's a shopping mall a five-minute
walk up the street if you'd rather walk,
miss," the taxi driver, a woman with fiery
red hair that had to be a dye-job, told Marie
with a smile. "You can get whatever you
want up there."

"Cool, thanks." A smile beamed back at
the driver as Marie slid from her seat.

"No problem. I'll help your fella get
these bags inside then. Welcome to Houston." The woman winked at Marie and disappeared behind the car.

"I hope you don't mind?" she asked
Anton as they walked away in the direction
of the mall.

"Not at all. I'd like to get a new phone for all of us, and a few other things that I'll be able to get there."

"Great. I think we'll need to take a taxi back but the walk is nice. At least there's no snow." She smiled at her bodyguard and he smiled back.

"We need sunglasses too, I can't believe we haven't got any of those either."

"There are things you don't think about until they're gone, you just take them for granted." Marie pulled the sleeves up on her sweater, but she was still too warm. A few minutes later they walked into a large mall and Marie stared around. "Okay, let's get a drink first, then clothes more suited to the weather."

"Good idea," Anton said, always a man of few words. He was in guard mode and kept an eye on everyone and everything as she walked up to the first shop that had bottles of water and got two for them. They drank the water as they walked into a clothing store. Marie immediately found several dresses, a pair of shorts, and several t-shirts. "Can I put this on and bring the tag out to you to pay for it?"

"Of course, missy," the thin young man with bleached blond hair and flirtatious eyes drawled. "You just go right on in the changing room and put that on before you roast to death. Just got into Texas have you?"

"Yes, I guess it's obvious." She looked down at herself and laughed.

"Just a little, but you'll fit right in. Go on in and change now, I'll be out here with this hunk you've got trailing behind you." He winked at Marie and she laughed happily.

She put on the dark-green strapless dress that swirled down to her ankles and put on the pair of strappy sandals she'd found to go with it. She felt much cooler and walked out of the changing room to pay. The salesman was obviously very interested in Anton, while Anton was busy blushing and trying to dissuade the young man from his attentions. The look of relief that came over Anton's face when she walked out was almost comical.

When he all but ran out of the store she had to tease him. "Anton, come back here. I think I've got your number on my phone if you want to give it to him."

"No," he murmured and ducked his head down.

"Come on, then, let's find some clothes for you and Matteo, then we can find food. That sandwich wasn't enough."

"Fine, but I'm not going back in that store."

"Oh, but I just remembered, I need another pair of shoes." His face was a picture of fear and she laughed. "I'm sorry, I'm only teasing. I'll stop now."

"Thank you," he whispered, but Marie heard him.

"Right. Jeans, shoes, boots maybe, shorts, did you get a basket? Oh, good, thanks." Marie took the deep basket and started to add things to it. By the time they were ready to go, she'd just started taking things to the counter. She found everything she needed for Matteo, Anton added to the pile, and they walked away with almost more bags than they could carry.

"One more stop," Anton said as he headed for an electronics store.

Marie waited with the extra bags but he wasn't gone long before he came back with even more bags.

"Can we carry all of this?" she asked, and he looked down at all of their new purchases. Marie looked at Anton and couldn't help but laugh at his helpless look. "Call a taxi and get room service at the hotel?"

"Good plan. I'll call the number from the other taxi."

When the car arrived outside the complex, Marie grinned to see it was the same woman. "We've been busy."

"I see that. Wow!" She was good-natured, not nasty, and Marie took it that way.

"I think there might be a couple of things left in there, but not many, if you need anything."

"That's nice of you." The driver loaded the bags into the car and then pulled out into traffic with Anton and Marie in the back. "Here we are."

It was only a two-minute drive for the woman, and most of that was spent at the stoplight in front of the mall.

"This one's on me, ma'am. It wasn't that much out of the way from where I was, and you've obviously had a problem lately. I'm not prying, just observing. You take care and I hope things get better for you all from here."

"Thanks, really."

"Take care now." The woman waved out of her window when she got back in after unloading the car again and drove away.

"She was really nice," Marie said to Anton and they carried the bags up to the room number Matteo had texted to them.

"She was," he agreed and knocked on the door.

Matteo opened the door, a smile on his face. "I ordered a pizza when you said you were getting a taxi. Room service is bringing it up when it's done. Apparently, it's huge and will feed us all."

Marie grinned, for the first time in days, she was relaxed and really happy.

# 21

---

Later that evening, Anton was in his room, playing with the new toys he'd found, and Marie was setting up her new phone. All of their new phones were pre-paid, so no contract, and they'd be able to use them in Mexico, he'd made sure of that too.

She found the same app she used to get books and Matteo gave her a debit card to use to open an account to order books with. She bought quite a few at once and downloaded them to her phone. It would be hard to say when they'd find new SIM cards and get them set up in Mexico so she did it all now.

The only numbers on the phone were his and Anton's but that was fine for now. She didn't want to talk to anyone else anyway.

"You doing alright, babe?" he asked as he prodded at the laptop Anton brought to him. He was using a VPN to access the files he needed to get some work done, things he had to approve for his many businesses, and some stuff for the family business. He'd also contacted a lawyer while they were gone and had set it up so that Trina would be the one to take over when he left the country.

"I'm fine, honey." She was trying to get one of the books to open but it wouldn't. She deleted it, then downloaded it again. It opened then and she sighed in satisfaction. "There we go."

"What was wrong?" he asked, absently.

"Nothing, my book didn't want to open, and I had to delete it and download it again."

"Ah, that old chestnut, huh? I hate it when you open it and the files are messed up. It's the same thing, though, delete it and download it again. It's a pain, but that's technology."

"Mmhmm," she murmured as an idea occurred to her. He looked so cute over there, his face so intent. There was a hottub in this room too, so she decided maybe it was time for some of her husband's attention.

"Matteo?" She took off her dress, her sandals were already in a corner of the room with their other purchases, and removed her underwear.

"What are you doing now?" She leaned over the tub, completely naked now, and turned the water on.

"Just some work, babe, be right with you." He didn't look up, and she got into the tub with a quiet smile and waited.

The sun had gone down an hour ago and the room was softly lit with only the light on the nightstand to chase the darkness away. When she turned the jets on, his head turned to look at her. She'd settled into the tub with only her breasts and upper torso out of the water. The water began to swirl around her and bubbles started to form.

"Oh," she heard him say as his eyes narrowed with hunger.

"Yes, I thought you might notice eventually." A grin twitched at her lips as he stood and pulled off the new t-shirt and pushed away from the shorts she'd bought him. She'd never seen him in shorts, but she liked it. He had thick calves and strong thighs that looked great.

"I have, indeed, noticed." He slid into the other end of the large tub and let the hot swirling water relax his muscles. "This was a really good idea."

"I thought so." She moved to slide up over him until she straddled his hips. "Hello, darlin', how are you?"

Her hips ground down into his as she

spoke, and he let his head fall back against the tub. "I'm heavenly, baby, just heavenly."

He was hard and ready already, so when she ground her slick skin against his, gently, it was pleasurable. For them both.

His hands came up straight into her hair, to pull her head to the right so he could take a bite at her neck. On that spot that she only let him touch. The spot that made her shiver over every inch of her body.

"Matteo," the name whispered from her lips as she braced herself with her arms on the sides of the tub. He thrust his hips against her center, buried beneath the water, between her folds, but not inside of her. Not yet.

"Say my name again, just like that, Marie. It's so pretty when you say it like that." He let her head go and brought his hands around to tilt her breasts up to his mouth.

Slowly, he teased each one, until she was a mess of thrusting hips and aching hunger.

She tried to touch herself but he wouldn't let her, wouldn't let her ease the hunger, not yet. "Matteo, please."

"No, baby, not yet." He went back to her other nipple, sucked it, flicked at it with his tongue until she was ready to jump out of the tub and relieve herself if he wouldn't do it.

She started to move, but one hand clamped on her hips kept her still, kept her on his dick. "I need you so much, I need to come."

"You can take more, darling, so much more. Enjoy it. Don't just reach for the end goal, enjoy the experience of getting there. For just a little while longer." He purred the instructions against her neck as he leaned up. His hand slid around to her ass, and he lifted them both out of the tub, somehow steady enough to step out and lay her on the carpeted floor.

"Relax, my love. Let me make you feel good." He pushed her legs apart, pulled her roughly against his mouth, and began to feast.

His name tore from her lips as her back arched and her hips twisted. She put a hand over her mouth as another cry, almost a scream, followed that. His tongue went straight to her clit, forcing her up quickly, so fucking quickly, before he moved, flipped her over, and got between her legs. He wasn't about to fuck her though. Not yet.

He raked his fingers down her back, his nails scratching at her lightly. She focused on the sensation as he did it again, and her hips bucked all over again. "Matteo."

It was a whisper, he barely even heard it, but it was there. His fingers moved down over her ass. She wanted to squirm away when he opened her up, but he pressed his hands down on her to hold her still. She knew she couldn't take this, not right now. He'd make her come if he touched her there.

His fingers came down to her pussy, before it moved up, slowly, to circle around her other entrance. "Open for me, Marie. Come on now, be good."

With a sigh of resignation, she did as he instructed, though all she wanted to do was grind her clit against anything; his hand, her hand, the floor, it didn't matter. When his finger pressed into her back entrance, when it slid *in* - fuck, oh fuck, it was so very *good*.

Shivers, more shivers, shivers that made her nipples go even tighter, that made her clit throb harder, that made the hunger deep inside even hungrier, swamped over her as his finger slid deeper into her.

"Your pussy is dripping, Marie, so ready for my cock." He made sure of that when he slid the fingers of his other hand into her. "You're so ready to be fucked baby, and I'm going to do it, alright? I'm going to fuck you so good, with my finger in your ass and my cock in those sweet walls that suck me in ways only your pussy does."

All she could do was whimper as he

guided her to her knees, his finger still deep inside of her backside. She groaned when he positioned his tip at her pussy, when he teased her with a swipe of his cock against her there, before he thrust in suddenly, all the way to the hilt.

"Fuck," she gasped. Her hands dug into the carpet. She was as full as he could get until he pulled his finger out of her ass. He wasn't done though. He licked his thumb and pushed that into her instead - a thicker digit, so much thicker, than his finger. He began to move that thumb in time with the thrust of his cock.

"Don't," Matteo ordered when she moved to touch herself, to end the aching misery of her hunger. "Not yet."

"When Matteo?" she pleaded, so hungry for it now.

"When you calm down, when you feel the pleasure of fucking, not just trying to reach an orgasm. Tell me how you feel." He slowed his thrusts as he spoke and she groaned with impatience.

"I feel… full. Hungry, like I need something, a drug, that only you can give me. Please, can't I come now?"

"Do you know how many women can't, Marie? You're lucky, you get to do this quite often. Some women never get to. But you will baby, don't worry, I'm going to make you come. Just concentrate on what you feel."

She tried. She paid attention to the sensation of her nipples scraping against the carpet, and suddenly it was good, it wasn't painful. It was a burn that added to the throb between her legs, which made her blood pulse even harder in her veins.

Every time he fucked into her she felt a soft touch against her clit, she felt the way he slapped against her ass as a new thing, as an intimate touch that she'd only ever shared with him. Even her arm became sensitive as she felt warm air touch her. The cool sensation of her hair against her hot face was almost soothing, but she didn't want to be soothed. She wanted to explode.

He pushed his thumb into her harder, faster until she was almost unconscious with her gasps of pleasure. And she still hadn't come, not yet. Not until she bent down, let her head rest against the floor, her knees still holding her ass up so that he could thrust down, to that spot that made the world disappear. She cried out then, a strangled sound that was barely a sound at all because she just had no air left.

She felt the explosion inside of her walls as she gripped at his cock. She felt it as an explosion of pleasurable bolts of electricity that shot from her clit, up her spine, through her stomach, and straight into her brain. She inhaled sharply, quickly, before the world went dark and pleasure made every inch of her skin contract. She came apart hard, so hard she pulled him with her. She heard it but didn't care, didn't care that he'd groaned in release, that he was right there with her, because everything was so... fucking... good.

She slumped to the floor, completely

done, and just let it wash over her as he pulled away to rest on the floor at her feet.

"See? It's so much better when you work for it, when you earn it, Marie. That's when it blows your fucking mind completely."

Her hand fluttered up in recognition of his words, but she couldn't answer. Not yet. She did smile though. Even if it was a tired one. He'd been right. Once again. As he always was. Smug fucker.

## 2 2

The phone buzzed in the middle of the night and woke Matteo up. He'd taken Marie to bed and wrecked her one more time before they fell asleep together. They hadn't even pulled the plug in the tub. They'd just fallen asleep twisted around each other. Now, his new phone buzzed. He looked at it to see it was Petey on Skype.

"Hey boss, sorry to wake you. I know it's still night there but I have news." The voice on the other end sounded tense, so tense Mattco sat up in bed.

"Okay. Tell me."

"It's her, your aunt. I have her in my sights, boss. Just tell me and I'll end her." Matteo could hear a gentle wind over the line and knew Petey was outside somewhere in Italy. With a sniper rifle, ready to earn his pay, however his boss told him to earn it.

"You're sure?" he asked, anger ice in his veins.

"Yes, I'm sure, Matteo. Got the document she put out to prove it." Petey sighed, not judging, just passing information.

"Okay. Let me make a call. Hang on, don't hang up."

"Sure, boss. I'll be right here. She's sunning herself by the pool, she ain't going nowhere."

"Okay."

He picked up his laptop, opened it up, and used his Google Hangouts number to call Celeste in Italy. It called her new cellphone number there, and he wasn't surprised when she picked it up.

"Matteo, I didn't expect to hear from

you." She didn't sound pleased about the call. He was about to make that displeasure even worse.

"You fucking sick bitch. I have proof it was you. And before you hang up, let me tell you, there's a sniper with your head in his sights right now. He can turn your head into a blown-up watermelon in seconds. So, don't hang up."

"Okay. I'm not sure what you're talking about, but I'm listening."

"You put the contract out on Marie, and then apparently me because Fiona fucking shot me." He growled and nearly lost his control, but it snapped back into place when Marie shifted, still asleep, but easing an ache.

"Matteo, she needed to go..." she started but he stopped her.

"Fuck you. You have two options, *Aunty*." He sneered the title at her. He hated her, he hated her so very much. "Either you take your medicine and eat a bullet for your lunch, or you leave the family, forever. You can have some of the money, your bullshit villa in Italy, and you leave us alone. We never see your face again. Any of us. I'm the king of this family now and you are done. Got me? Because if you go back against your word, your head will explode the second I find out about it, am I clear?"

"Yes, Matteo. I'll have the paperwork sent to the lawyer. It's all yours. I guess I did well. You've taken what I wanted to give you. Keep your little strumpet. I'll stay over here and enjoy my retirement knowing you're the man I raised you to be. Well done, my boy." She tittered out a laugh, but he could hear the way her voice shook. She was terrified.

"Fuck you. Don't come near any of us again and call off the contract. Now. If my man doesn't see you on the phone in the next five minutes, you're dead, understand?"

"Yes, Matteo. I'm, I'm sorry."

"Again, fuck you. Goodbye." He cut the

line and went back to the phone where Petey waited for his orders.

"Well, what's she doing now?"

"Apparently, pissing herself and screaming for a phone."

"Good, watch her. I'll wait." It was almost over. Relief flooded through him; it was almost done. Marie would be able to walk out in public again. Thank fuck, this was almost over.

He felt his entire body begin to shake but took a deep breath and pushed away his body's response to relief. His free hand went to Marie's hip, held her, and took comfort from her presence.

"She's calling someone. Hang on, my other phone is ringing." Petey answered the other line, and Matteo could hear him. "It's done, is it? Canceled? Good, she gets to live then. Smart woman."

He said a few things more, told the man to get the info to America, quickly, as in now. He didn't care who had to be woken up, get the contract canceled. "Boss, you still there?"

"Yes. It's done then?" He loved technology in that instant. The news would travel in minutes now. Around the globe at the stroke of a key. Fucking awesome.

"It's done. You can come out now."

"Actually, I think I might take my wife on a little bit of a real vacation." He chuckled and thought about the RV. Anton could go home, but he might stay if Matteo asked him to, as security while they traveled in Mexico.

"You do whatever you want to, boss. You can now." Petey laughed. "I'll call you later on. Get back to sleep now, knowing she's safe."

"I will, Petey, thank you." Matteo slid down in the bed as the call ended, and he pulled Marie into his arms. "It's over, my love."

"What?" she asked sleepily, her head on his chest. She snored again and he laughed softly.

"Come on, baby, wake up a little. Celeste has called off the contract. We can come out of hiding now."

"What? What time is it?" She sat up and looked at the clock on the nightstand. "It's 6 am, Matteo, couldn't you let me sleep an hour more?"

"No, not really. I probably should, but it couldn't wait. I'm going to get Anton up too. Our plans might change." He called his bodyguard and the man came to the room at once.

"Does he ever sleep?" Marie wondered as Matteo opened the door.

"It's done. Petey found out it was Celeste, got her in his rifle's sights, and she called it off. It's being spread now, the word that it's over at least."

"That's great news! We can go back to New York." He smiled and looked at them both with happiness. "Or are we heading to Mexico for a week or two anyway?"

"I thought, while we were down here, we might as well, right?"

"Right. Totally right," Marie agreed and jumped out of bed. "I'll call room service."

"And I'll call that lady with the taxi." Anton checked the time. "Does eight sound good? We can all eat, shower, whatever, pack up, and be downstairs by then."

"That works," Matteo answered as Anton went out to arrange for the taxi on the balcony.

Marie put the phone down, the breakfast she'd ordered for them all this morning a little healthier, and grinned at Matteo. "We're free."

"We are. Both of us." He took a deep breath and sat down with her on the bed. "How do you feel?"

"Like the world has been lifted from my shoulders," she sighed out; her eyes closed. "Like I can think again without every thought being formed from fear."

"You've been so brave, Marie. Braver than you should have had to be. I'm so proud of you." He kissed her, but Anton came back in, so they parted with secret smiles. Later, they'd continue that kiss.

"Taxi will be here at eight on the dot and I just saw the room service trolley come out of the elevator." A knock at the door proved him right. He let them in and two trollies rolled in, with bowls of cut fruit, oatmeal, and toast.

It wasn't the breakfast that mattered though, it was the feeling as each one let it sink in that it was all over that mattered. Laughs broke out spontaneously or sighs as each one came to the same conclusion. It was done. Whatever came next was done for fun.

Matteo was ready for a real vacation. As he looked at his wife, he decided that soon he'd tell her the one thing he'd held back. Those three little words that would make her never stop smiling. Soon.

THEY STAYED in Mexico for one week, each day in a new place before they had to fly Marie back to New York. She'd fallen and her right leg had started to tremble. It had scared all of them so they arranged for someone to pick up the RV and flew directly back home. Matteo drove her to the hospital straight from the airport and her doctor met them there.

"You had a fall, you said?" the doctor asked as Marie began to list things that had been going on lately. They spoke for a while and the doctor sat on the side of her bed while he spoke to her.

Matteo watched from the chair at her bedside, waiting to hear what the doctor would say. "Right, I know where you're heading with this and yes, I agree, we need to run some tests on you. As you're so young, I'd like to do genetic testing, to see if there are any mutations there, with your permission? It will aid current studies going on. I'll have some blood taken for other blood work too, and someone will be up soon to do a CT scan on your brain. That will show us if there are signs of the disease in your brain. Don't worry, the worst part will be getting the IV."

"Right. Thanks, doctor." Marie smiled vaguely, her eyes worried. She looked over at Matteo, heartbreak in her eyes. They'd been having so much fun in Mexico: drinking, eating, exploring, it had all been fun, and then she fell, completely sober, and gave herself a nasty scalp laceration that had needed stitches. She'd just been standing there, talking with Anton, and had been about to turn to talk to Matteo when she just... fell over.

He could see the pain in her eyes, the heartbreak, and could all but see her thoughts. She'd have to leave him, have to run away, but he wouldn't let her. Whatever happened, he was her husband. He would take care of her for the rest of his life.

"I'll be back later. The nurse will come in soon and get that IV in, alright?"

Marie nodded and inhaled deeply. "Well,

I think we know what the answer is going to be don't we?"

"I have to admit, he sounds like he's leaning that way too, Marie." He was the one that sighed this time. "I'll be here for you, okay? You don't have to go through this alone."

"I know." Tears broke her voice and fell from her eyes and he was up at once, holding her in his arms as she sobbed on his chest.

He brushed hair away from her face and looked into her eyes. "I'll comb the world to find something, anything you need, do you understand me? I don't care if it takes all of our money, you won't suffer like your mother, hear me?"

"I do, Matteo, I do." She nodded her head against his chest and pulled away as the nurse came in. "Hi."

"Hi there, sweetie. I'm going to put your IV in, alright? For now, we're just going to run saline into you to make sure you're hydrated, then we'll take some blood. Then radiology will be up in an hour or so to take you down for your scans, that's why I have to put in such a large IV. This is going to hurt a little, so be brave for me, okay? I'm sorry, but it has to be done." The nurse was a red-haired woman with kind green eyes, probably in her 60s, so that reassured Marie, and Matteo too. She had the experience, at least.

Marie held her arm out like a trooper, and the nurse was right, the IV hurt, but Marie only gasped and bit down on her lip. It was a long night that turned into two days before the doctor finally had enough evidence to make a diagnosis. He'd come in periodically to check on Marie, but on that last day, he came in with a rather solemn look on his face.

That look said their entire world was about to change. Again. Fuck. Matteo felt a crushing weight in his chest and took Marie's hand. He couldn't imagine how she felt. Her face hid it all as the doctor began to speak.

"Right, there is really no definitive test to diagnose Parkinson's disease but we found a couple of genetic mutations we expect to find with Parkinson's, and your brain shows some signs of Parkinson's. I'm sorry, Marie, but my conclusion is that you do have Parkinson's. I checked everything else it could be, my dear, and I tried to find another explanation for you, but the scan of your brain with those mutations? Well, it's fairly clear. I'll be here every step of the way through, and we'll give you medication that will control a lot of the symptoms you're having. It won't stop it, but the medicine will help."

He paused to let the news sink and looked at them both in turn. "Any questions?"

They both just shook their heads and tried to process the diagnosis. They'd both suspected it for a long time and Marie had already started to cope with the idea of it, but to know for sure, well, that was different. Matteo watched her, ready to go to her at any sign of tears, but instead, she smiled at the doctor. Smiled. He was stunned.

"I think I know more about what to expect than anyone else might, so no, I don't have any questions for now. Oh, I do have one. What about my children?"

"It's hard to tell, Marie. I couldn't say yes, your children will be fine, or no they won't be. It's a crapshoot with genetics. I'm sorry I can't offer more hope than that." He patted her hand and turned to leave but looked back. "I'll release you today, so you can go home and get some rest. I'm going to recommend physical therapy now, the earlier we start it, the better."

"Thanks, doctor," Matteo said and looked back at his wife. She was still smiling, despite the news about children. "You amaze me, you know that?"

"Well, it's those stages of grief, isn't it? I've come to a point where I can accept it. Maybe later I'll fall back into depression or denial, I don't know. But for now, I feel good. I know now, and I can cope with that."

"Can you?" He'd expected tears, screams maybe, for her to run away and never come back out of some kind of sense of being the better person. Or some shit like that. Instead, she beamed at him.

"We know now. We can cope. I know you want me with you now. You ran across the country, into another country, got shot, and almost, well, took care of your aunt for me. You may not have said it, Matteo, but you showed me. You did something nobody else has ever done for me and showed me that you love me. Like I love you." Her eyes went wide as she said those words, almost as if she was afraid, but he leaned in to look at her.

"You love me?" His eyes were as wide as hers.

"I do, Matteo. I love you more than anything else in this world. More than I thought was possible. I love you so much it would kill me if I wasn't with you. It's insane really. I thought I'd end up alone, but here I am, in love with you."

"I'd follow you to the edges of the universe, Marie. I'd burn the entire world down for you. But I think I've proven that by now."

"You have, Matteo." She took a deep breath and looked away for a minute, her face tense. "I hated having to marry you to take care of a debt. I hated being coerced into it, but now, well, I still hate it, but I'm glad I did it now. I really am."

"Good, because I do love you, Marie. More than I could ever show you. If I prove it every day for the rest of my life, I still couldn't show you how much I love you."

"You do it every day, Matteo. Whether you know it or not, you do." She sat up straight, took a deep breath, and spoke again. "Now, let's go out and live the rest of our lives, shall we?"

"I'd love to, Marie, I'd love to."

# 23

Two years later...

"We have to go, Matteo, now." Marie shoved at her sleeping husband, excited and filled with wonder already. Her babies were on their way.

They'd found the perfect surrogate and she'd donated her eggs, used Matteo's sperm, and now they had a daughter and a son on the way. The surrogate had called her - she was in active labor at the hospital.

It had been a long process; Marie had thought it over, talked it over with Matteo for a year. Research showed that pregnancy makes the Parkinson's symptoms worse, and with her genetic mutations, they finally came to the agreement that they'd find a surrogate if they could. They'd been lucky with the woman they chose. She donated the eggs, and she looked similar to Marie so maybe the babies would look a little like her. Her name was Mariella too, so it almost seemed like fate when they found her.

Matteo finally woke up and blinked his way down to the stairs of their new home in a quiet neighborhood that didn't constantly hum on the outskirts of New York City. There was a nursery and two rooms that would be theirs when they were old enough to have their own beds.

Trina met them at the hospital, her face as excited as Marie's. "I'm here, oh my goodness, how is she doing?"

"I don't know, we just got here too. Come on."

They all marched down to the room Mariella was in and stood in the doorway. The young woman looked up at them, her face wreathed in pain, but happy. "Don't just stand there, come hold my hand!"

Marie and Trina laughed and went in. Matteo hung out at the end of the room he was paying for, a private labor room, and put his head down, just like she used to see Anton doing. He was suddenly shy. She'd have laughed if Mariella hadn't just squeezed her hand in a vice.

"Push, Mariella. Baby one is almost out," the doctor peering between the surrogate's thighs said.

Mariella pushed until she screamed, but their little boy slipped out of her body at 6:57 am, perfect and healthy. A half-hour later, their baby girl was born, with all her fingers and toes, a little sluggish, but she soon perked up.

"They're perfect, Mariella. Oh my goodness. Thank you so much." Marie rained kisses down on the young woman's head.

"I don't plan to have any of my own, as you know, but I wanted to have the experience. I could gift someone that experience, and I chose you. You two will be perfect for these two babies. I know it."

"You don't regret it?" Marie asked the hard question that had worried her so much.

"No, I don't. I might later, I can't swear I won't, but you guys are going to keep in touch, right? You don't plan to just disappear. And anyway, legally, they're yours now. Even after this, I don't think I'll want to have children of my own, but you at least let me have the experience, so thank you." Mariella, her face a little swollen, smiled, perfectly happy with the world.

She was right, though, the babies were legally theirs now. Marie would be listed as the mother, and Matteo was definitely the father. She saw his gray eyes when she looked at their daughter once the nurses handed her over. His chin was there on their son's face when she took that baby too. Trina, almost more excited than the new parents, snapped a picture that would become all of their favorite because Marie was beaming so brightly it was almost goofy, but they didn't care. She was happy and that's all any of them wanted. To give Marie as much joy in life as she could get.

"Did you decide on their names?" Mariella asked.

"Well, if you don't mind, I'd like to name her Mariella, after you. She's going to know you as an aunt, and we can call her Ella for short. And he's going to be Antonio, after Mommy's favorite fella, after his daddy."

"Those are wonderful names." Mariella smiled tears of happiness in her eyes.

Marie had been impressed with her from the start. She was 25, completely healthy, and wanted to experience pregnancy and birth, but didn't want to raise children. She'd had a rough childhood, something that she and Marie had bonded over. She'd become a friend, and when she met Trina, it was as if the trio was complete and she'd fit right in.

Marie worried that once her hormones settled and she spent some time with the babies, she'd change her mind. But at the same time, she'd come to know Mariella. That experience told her the woman wouldn't change her mind. She knew these were Marie's babies, she'd always said it. Legality aside, they'd been conceived for Marie, not Mariella, and Mariella was definite about that.

Matteo took his babies in his arms and instantly fell in love, just as much as their mother had. The second photo proved it when it was sent to the happy new parents. Mariella and Antonio, their children, their babies.

"Our family is complete now, Matteo," she whispered as she stood over the chair where he sat as he held the babies. "We have it all, all we could ever want."

"We have a healthy, stable you, two

healthy babies, and each other. Yeah, you're right. That's all we need. And I will protect all three of you with every fiber of my being."

"Oh my God, I'm going to die from the diabetes I catch from you two." Trina pretended to gag as she walked over to Mariella. "Can you believe people go that gooey over babies?"

"Fuck off, Trina. I saw your face when Antonio was born! You were in love," Matteo said quietly, with a hint of laughter.

"You're all going to make me gag if you don't stop." Mariella laughed as she tried to move around. Trina was there instantly to help her. Mariella had needed stitches and had to be careful. Trina would be her support for the next few days, and Marie and Matteo would be on call too if she needed them. Trina, however, would be there for the surrogate mother when she went home, she would help her as she healed up and recovered.

"When can we take them home?" Matteo asked the nurse that came in.

"Well, if the doctor clears them, probably tonight. If not, a couple of days usually. They're healthy and doing well, so I don't see a problem."

"Oh, really?" Matteo looked at Marie in panic. "We didn't bring their car seats."

They had a new SUV, just for the babies, and he'd not put their seats in yet. They were a week early, after all.

"We can get them, honey, don't freak out." Marie was busy giving her daughter a bottle when the nurse brought it in, and Trina was feeding Antonio.

A nanny would show up at the house when Marie called her, she'd been on standby for a week now, just in case. Marie had wanted the nanny just as a helper, not as the woman that would raise the babies, but she knew her mother had barely coped with her. Secretly, she had fears that she wouldn't be a good mother, but from the moment she saw her children, it was obvious she wasn't her mother at all. Plus, it would be nice to have someone to help her and Matteo with the babies.

They could afford it, so why not, she'd finally figured.

Marie looked down at her little Ella's face and couldn't believe the baby was hers, all hers. "You know," she whispered to the little girl, "you're already more than I could have hoped for."

The baby clutched at her finger as Marie held her bottle, her eyes unfocused, still that newborn blue that so many babies were born with. Later, they would change into a different shade, either Mariella's brown or Matteo's grey, maybe some other shade in their DNA, but Marie didn't care. They were her babies, and she loved them already.

"I'm going to be the best mom I can be to you and your brother, Ella. I promise that. You won't ever know any of the fear or the pain I had. I will fight tooth and nail to make sure of that. Never." She kissed the baby's head and felt an ache that she'd thought had disappeared long ago start to ease. Tears filled her eyes, and she almost sobbed she was so overwhelmed.

She'd kept it secret for so long, how afraid she was that she'd be terrible at this, that she'd feel the same hate her mother had felt when she'd seen Marie the first time. But it hadn't been like that. It was the opposite, and for the first time, she truly knew it wasn't her fault her mother hated her. There'd been something wrong with Ruby, something that was broken long before Marie came along and it wasn't her fault at all.

"What's wrong, honey?" Matteo knelt down and wiped at her tears. "Why are you crying?"

"Because I'm in love, Matteo. I was so afraid that it wouldn't happen, but it's there. I feel it. So much love. An enormous amount of love that's chasing so much pain away. It's amazing." She cried even harder, but then laughed. "I'm sorry, I'll explain it later."

"I think I understand. We're both kind of in the same boat, aren't we? Our parents weren't the best, and that's part of the reason I agreed to a nanny. We have no clue how to be good parents, other than what the books have said, or what we would have wanted. Instinct is a great teacher, I think. We'll figure this out. Besides, most people have no clue how to be good parents, even with all the books. I think, as long as we show them that we love them, raise them to be good people, and to be strong, then we'll do alright, don't you?"

"I think so. Oh boy. The doctor's coming back already." They'd been there for hours, but Marie hadn't noticed. The time had slipped away between feedings, diaper changes, and taking care of Mariella.

"Can I have her, Mrs. Mazza?" a nurse

asked, a smile in place as she took Ella away. "The doctor wants to check her one more time before he agrees they can go home."

"Maybe we should leave them in for one night?" Marie said, suddenly worried.

"If there's no need to, it'll be fine, Mrs. Mazza. I promise," the nurse said reassuringly.

Marie couldn't wrap her head around it, that they'd be released so soon, but there it was. Experts knew better than her.

Mariella would stay in for at least one more day, but the babies were healthy and thriving, the doctor decided. If they wanted to take them home, it would be perfectly fine. They'd filled out the paperwork earlier to apply for birth certificates and whatever else it was. It was all a blur to Marie now and she had no clue what she'd signed and what she hadn't. There'd been a lawyer at one point, to ensure everything was done legally, and then he left. Now, the babies were in their car seats, and ready to go home.

"Mariella, are you sure you're alright?" Marie paused to ask. The young woman beamed at her.

"I'm fine, Marie. I swear. Don't worry. Those are all your babies. You're their mommy and Matteo is their daddy. And I'll be fine, I have Trina here to keep me company." She waved at them and went on. "Go home now, enjoy your babies."

Marie rushed over to her, kissed her cheek, and then walked out with her new baby in a car seat. Matteo had Ella and Marie had Antonio, both tucked under a blanket.

"They're so tiny, Matteo, are you sure about this? What if they get sick?"

"They won't, Marie, and tonight they'll sleep in bassinets in our room. Tomorrow when the nanny comes, they'll go to the nursery, but they will not be alone for a moment from now on. Well, until we get used to this."

Marie helped him to buckle the twins into the backseat and put the diaper bag on the floor of the SUV on the driver's side. "You okay to let me drive?"

"I am. You've come along with your driving up here. It's brave, but then you're always brave, aren't you?" He looked tired but happy, pleased even. He had a son and a daughter. And her.

"You know, I was terrified my past would come back to haunt me, would rule my life when they came along, but I don't feel like that anymore. I make my present, I make the future, and what happens from now on is up to us, isn't it?"

"It is, Marie, but you know that now. We're in this together and our babies, our lives, are ours to guide. We might get knocked back by life or something else, but I know one thing: they will not end up with a woman like Celeste, and you and I will love them into being two incredible people."

Celeste. She'd disappeared in Tibet and

nobody had heard from her since. That was probably the most sensible thing that woman ever did. "And they won't know a woman like my mother. Thank fuck."

"Now, Marie. The babies can hear you," Matteo chided in jest.

"We're going to have to watch that now, aren't we?"

"We are, but you know something that's really, really great about surrogacy?" he asked before she pulled into their driveway and stopped the car. "We don't have to wait six weeks to have sex."

"Fucking hell, Matteo, you're incorrigible." But she grinned. She grinned so wide. Her medicine was working, she was on birth control, and she rarely, if ever, had a tremor now. She had a good few years, at least, so she was looking forward to the future. A future with a husband that still wanted her like he'd only just met her. He loved her completely, and now, they had their babies. It was more than she could have asked for. But it was what she deserved, she decided as they took the babies up to their nursery and settled in with them. She and Matteo deserved this happiness, together.

THE END

# ALSO BY SUMMER COOPER

Read Summer's sexiest and most popular romance books.

**DARK DESIRES SERIES**
Dark Desire
Dark Rules
Dark Secret
Dark Time
Dark Truth

**An Amazon Top 100**
A sexy romantic comedy
Somebody To Love

## An Amazon Top 100
A 5-book billionaire romance box set
Filthy Rich
Summer's other box sets include:
Too Much To Love
Down Right Dirty

## Mafia's Obsession
A hot mafia romance series
Mafia's Dirty Secret
Mafia's Fake Bride
Mafia's Final Play

## Screaming Demons
An MC romance series full of suspense
*Take Over*
Rough Start
Rough Ride
Rough Choice
*New Era*
Rough Patch
Rough Return
Rough Road
*New Territory*

Rough Trip
Rough Night
Rough Love

Check out Summer's entire collection at
**www.summercooper.com/books**

Happy reading,
Summer Cooper
xoxo

# ABOUT SUMMER COOPER

Thank you so much for reading. Without you, it wouldn't be possible for me to be a full-time author. I hope you enjoy reading my books as much as I do writing them.

Besides (obviously!) reading and writing, I also love cuddling my dogs, shouting at Alexa, being upside down (aka Yoga) and driving my family cray-cray!

Follow me on
Facebook | Instagram
Goodreads | Bookbub | Amazon

Get in touch at
hello@summercooper.com

www.summercooper.com

Made in the USA
Coppell, TX
19 August 2021